Mom's Choice Silver Award Winner

What early readers are s

"A uniquely captivating and dazzling adventure into the reaches of inner and outer space. A wonderful, valuable read for both children and adults alike!"

-Angelica Kaner, PhD - Psychologist/Psychoanalyst, New Haven CT

"Finally, an author who helps us understand that we sculpt society to meet the needs of our children and not the other way around. This work is a heart-warming journey of growth, understanding and celebration!"

-Melissa Schlenker, MS - Middle school counselor, Sacramento CA

"Entertaining and intriguing! This book is so good you can't put it down. I finished it in one night! If you love adventures, you will love this book."

-Paige, age 11, grade 6

"If you are a Harry Potter fan, you are going to love this book! It is the most creative adventure story I have read in a long, long time. Even after I finished the book, I couldn't stop thinking about the characters and the story. It really makes you think. I can't wait for the next book to come out!!"

-Hana, age 11, grade 6

MATEO

AND THE
Gift of Presence

RUTHY BALLARD

Spinning Wheel Press
Sacramento, California

Spinning Wheel Press
P.O. Box 19481
Sacramento, CA 95819
www.SpinningWheelPress.com

Copyeditor: Lisa Canfield, www.copycoachlisa.com and
     Michelle Hershberger
Book design: Davis Creative, DavisCreative.com

Publisher's Cataloging-In-Publication Data
(Prepared by The Donohue Group, Inc.)

Names: Ballard, Ruthy.
Title: Mateo and the Gift of Presence / Ruthy Ballard.
Description: Sacramento, California; Spinning Wheel Press, [2017] | Series: [Tales by Moons-Light™] | Interest age level: 008-012. | Summary: "Laid-back Mateo Marino doesn't brood about the past or worry about the future. Instead, he lives in the present moment, driving his high-achieving parents crazy. Mateo feels unseen and unappreciated, especially compared to his younger brother, Alex. But everything changes when Mateo disappears through a mysterious crack in his bedroom ceiling and finds himself on a planet called Urth, 67,000 light years away." — Provided by publisher.
Identifiers: LCCN 2016911781 | ISBN 978-0-9978532-0-9 (paperback) | ISBN 978-0-9978532-2-3 (mobi) | ISBN 978-0-9978532-3-0 (ePub)
Subjects: LCSH: Boys—Outer space—Juvenile fiction. | Missing persons—Juvenile fiction. | Planets—Juvenile fiction. | Parent and child—Juvenile fiction. | Self-actualization (Psychology)—Juvenile fiction. | Awareness—Juvenile fiction. | CYAC: Boys—Outer space—Fiction. | Missing persons—Fiction. | Planets—Fiction. | Parent and child—Fiction. | Self-actualization (Psychology)—Fiction. | Awareness—Fiction. | LCGFT: Science fiction. | Action and adventure fiction.
Classification: LCC PZ7.1.B35 Ma 2017 (print) | LCC LCC PZ7.1.B35 (ebook) | DDC [Fic]--dc23

Published in the U.S.A.

For Sleeli, who has the gift of *Looking Closely,*
and for special children of all ages
and the people who love them.

Table of Contents

GLOSSARY

(Note: Terms defined elsewhere in the Glossary are indicated by italics.)

Alex Marino: *Mateo Marino's* "perfect" younger brother.

Anagram: a word, phrase, or name formed by rearranging the letters of another, such as *cinema*, formed from *iceman*.

A Traveler's Guide to Urth: A comprehensive textbook that includes anatomically correct drawings of *urthlings*.

August Slepe: *Jimmy Oscar Albini's* deadbeat, incompetent defense attorney.

Bob's Roofing: The business where *Jimmy Oscar Albini* works as an expert roofer.

Cairntip Island: The largest island on *Urth*. The center of trade and commerce and *Ideth's* home.

Celestia: A planet, similar to Earth's Venus, that shines brightly in *Urth's* morning or evening skies and has three moons.

Chatterboxes: Cell phone-like devices that *urthlings* used for communication before the *great melt*.

CODIS: A national database of DNA profiles from known criminals that can be used to identify the perpetrator of a crime.

Ducky sack: A very comfortable sleeping bag stuffed with the feathers of a *Cairntip* Doow Duck.

Doow Duck: An urth duck with amazingly soft and insulating feathers. Used to make *ducky sacks*.

Duppies: *Urthlings* who live on *training islands* and help *uppies* train their *findlings*. Every *finding* requires one *uppy* and several or more duppies.

Elvia (EL-VEE-UH): A *findling* with the gift of Feeling Deeply. Elvia is about to start her adventure while *Mateo Marino* is finishing his.

Earth Year (EY): The 365 day period it takes earth to revolve around the sun. One earth year is equal to two *urth years* (*UY*).

East End Paddling Station: An underwater hotel where *uppies* sometimes take their *findlings* on the way to and from their *training islands*. Sometimes called "The East Ender" for short.

Echolocation: A navigation system used by *urthlings* while *paddling*. It involves emitting sound waves and detecting their echoes to determine where objects are in deep and murky waters.

Finding: The process of training an *unseen child*. A finding begins on *Finding Island*, where the *unseen child* first appears on *urth*, and ends on *Returning Island*, where the child is sent home.

Finding Island: The island where uppies go to find their *findlings*.

Findling: An *unseen child* who is on a *finding* with his *uppy*.

Flare: A type of pyrotechnic (firework) that produces a brilliant light or intense heat without an explosion. On *urth*, flares are used as a form of communication over long distances, especially at sea.

Flareman: A person (not necessarily a man) who watches for *flares* sent up by *uppies* who have found their *findlings* and are ready to leave *Finding Island*.

Gift: A natural strength or inclination. Every child has one. Examples: Forging New Paths, Loving Numbers, Liking Spiders.

Great melt: A catastrophic event on *Urth* when the ice cap glaciers melted, the sea levels rose, and the planet lost all its great continents. The great melt happened very quickly and many generations before *Mateo Marino's* arrival. It reduced *urth's* landmasses to a set of widely distributed islands.

Hands: *Jimmy Oscar Albini's* nickname when he was in a gang.

Ideth: Grandmotherly-like *urthling* woman who is *Mateo Marino's uppy*.

Iktae: *Shum's* shy and book-loving young daughter.

Jimmy Oscar Albini: Innocent man accused of *Mateo Marino's* abduction.

King Pin: The leader of *Jimmy Oscar Albini's* gang who appreciates Jimmy's gift of Liking to Do Things Well. After Jimmy gets out of the gang and is living a lonely life, he names his cat after him.

Krog Pad Island: *Mateo Marino's training island.*

Krog Padders: The residents of *Krog Pad Island.*

Krog Pad dialect: An abbreviated form of English spoken by *Krog Padders.*

Lacie: *Elvia's* gorgeous *uppy.*

Laup: A *flareman* who meets *Mateo Marino* and *Ideth* on *Finding Island* and stocks them for their trip to *Krog Pad Island.*

Light year: The distance light travels in one year. It is nearly 6 trillion miles.

Lila: A drop-dead gorgeous young assistant for *Maria Thomson* whom *Jimmy Oscar Albini* asks on a date and eventually marries.

Lunera: The larger and brighter of *Urth's* two moons.

Maria Thomson: A manipulative reporter who tries to sensationalize *Jimmy Oscar Albini's* unjust incarceration.

Mateo Marino: An *unseen child* with the gift of Presence. He is the 10-year-old protagonist of the story.

Meato: Mateo's *rename.*

Moons-light: The light cast by two moons.

Moons-shadow: A fuzzy shadow created by the light of two moons.

Neap Tides: Mild (almost motionless) tides that occur when *Urth's* moons and sun balance one another's pulls on the planet.

Officer Morgan: Insensitive police officer leading the investigation into *Mateo Marino's* mysterious disappearance from Earth.

Paddle-saddlers: Fast-swimming *urthlings* who carry messages and mail between islands.

Paddling: *Urthling* word for swimming. *urthlings* are adapted to life by the ocean and can paddle long distances with minimal effort. They can *echolocate* to navigate in murky or deep waters and can hold their breaths for more than half an hour.

Rename: An *anagram* of a child's name. *Urth* children rename themselves around the age of 16 *(UY)* and have more control over their lives afterwards. *Findlings* also choose a rename during their *findings*.

Returning Island: The island where *uppies* take their *findlings* when they are ready to return them to Earth.

Roberto and Evelyn Marino: *Mateo Marino's* hard-driving parents who have lofty ambitions for him.

Ru: The smaller and dimmer of *Urth's* two moons.

Sarah: A kind young woman who rejects *Jimmy Oscar Albini's* invitation for a date.

Shum: One of *Mateo Marino's* loveable *duppies*. Shum's people live on *Krog Pad Island*.

Smusare Fiddle: Urth's premier astronomer who runs the Ilck Observatory on *Cairntip Island* and keeps track of the behavior of the moons and tides.

Stella Knight: The prim DNA expert who provides incriminating testimony at *Jimmy Oscar Albini's* trial.

Stripe: A "degree" earned by an *uppy* that enables him/her to find an *unseen child*. Each uppy stripes in one or more gifts that match the gifts of the children they are allowed to find.

Syzygy (SIZZ-UH-GEE): An astronomical event when *Urth* and its two moons are positioned in a straight line. *Urth's* tides are extreme during syzygies.

<u>Tales by Moons-Light: Stories from Before the Great Melt</u>: A beloved book read by all *urthling* children.

<u>The Art of Roofing</u>: The best-selling book that *Jimmy Oscar Albini* writes after he is freed from prison.

<u>The Good Urth</u>: A cookbook that *Mateo Marino* uses to teach *Iktae* to read.

Training Island: An island where a *findling* is trained.

Trilogy: A *syzygy* in which Urth's two moons and its sun are lined up on the same side of the planet. The moons are both new during a trilogy and the nights are very dark and filled with stars.

Uncle Alonzo: *Mateo Marino's* ne'er-do-well uncle, who is always asking *Roberto Marino* for money.

Unseen child: An earth child whose *gift* is not appreciated by his/her parents.

Uppies: Special *urthlings* who train *unseen children*.

Uppy Academy: Elite schools where *uppies* earn their *stripes*.

Uppy Council: Governing body that oversees the activities of *uppies*.

Urth: An Earth-like planet on the other side of the Milky Way galaxy. *Unseen children* are sometimes drawn there by a mysterious force.

Urthling: Humanoid-like beings who live on *Urth*. They have lavender skin, webbed feet, and a layer of indigo blubber around their midsections.

Urth Year (UY): The length of time it takes for *Urth* to revolve around its sun. One UY is half the length of one *earth year (EY)*.

Watler: A trader that Mateo and Ideth meet at the *East End Paddling Station*.

PROLOGUE

Mateo Marino was no ordinary boy. He was an *unseen* boy, which made all the difference. He wasn't invisible, or anything like that, though sometimes he thought he was. Instead, his parents looked straight through him, at the child they wanted him to be, missing altogether the boy that he was. And while it was sad, it was also wonderful. For children like Mateo can have adventures of the most extraordinary kind, and that's what happened to him. When he was ten years old, he disappeared, as unseen children sometimes do. And that's when everything changed, and why I have this tale to tell.

—The Narrator

Chapter 1

THE CRACK

There once was a boy named Mateo who lived in a fine house by the sea in a town called Monterey. The house had five bedrooms, a cozy family room full of books and pictures, and a sunny kitchen. There were two cats, Bigfoot and Yeti, and a hyperactive dog named Vortex. There was plenty of good food to eat, too, and Mateo ate plenty, fueling his naturally athletic body at every opportunity. In fact, he could have run around a baseball diamond and thrown a ball faster and farther than any of his friends, if he'd wanted to.

But Mateo was not like the other boys. Nor was he like his hard-driving, well-meaning parents who had lofty ambitions for him. Instead, Mateo liked to sit around and do nothing, or at least what looked like nothing to everyone else but was, in fact, something quite special.

You see, Mateo had *Presence*, which is a rare and wonderful gift indeed. He didn't brood about the past or plan for the future. Instead, he hung out in the present moment. And what did he do there? Well, I'll tell you. He *imagined*, which, to him, was much more fun than anything he was supposed to be doing.

Why play baseball for his school team when he could play hyper-baseball on the moon? There, home-runs soared several miles and the members of the opposing team had transparent skin and slithered around like snakes. Why work hard to make top grades (like his younger brother Alex did) when he could ski across Greenland with a pack of friendly wolves? They didn't care whether he could read, write, or do enough math to pass the boring standardized tests his teachers seemed so worried about. Why should he clean his room, help his mother with the dishes, feed the animals, take out the trash, or do any of the other hopelessly dull chores that his parents insisted that he do (and yelled at him when he didn't)? He had invisible friends to play with, up inside his head, who had bicycles with wings.

"You'll never amount to anything! You're just too LAZY and SELF-ABSORBED!" his father often scolded him. "You have so much potential, Mateo, but you're wasting it! If you keep this up you'll turn out just like your Uncle Alonzo, back in Italy, living off the family fat!"

His mother was equally concerned, but she tended to cajole rather than yell.

"Come on, Mateo, I know you can solve this math problem," she might say encouragingly. "Just apply yourself a little harder. And stop fiddling with your pencil. It's not a sword, you know."

Of course, to Mateo, the pencil *was* a sword—or at least it could be! And slaying a dragon with it would be much more exciting than using it to do his math homework.

"What are we going to do about him?" his parents constantly asked each other. "How can we get him motivated to succeed? He'll never get into college, much less a good college. When he's all grown up, he won't be able to get a job. He'll be homeless and lying in a gutter somewhere. There must be a way of making him see sense."

But there was nothing they could do. Not even the little yellow pills prescribed by their physician seemed to help. What bothered other people just didn't bother Mateo. College was years in the future and had no meaning for him. And getting the kind of dreary adult job his parents had in mind? Why would he ever want to do that when he could flip helium burgers on Jupiter or rule a kingdom of mermen in the Caspian Sea? Living in his imagination, he didn't have to lift a finger.

Threats like "Finish your homework or you won't get any dinner!" or "Get dressed for ball practice right now or you'll be grounded for a whole week!" didn't work either. Mateo had stopped listening a long time ago.

"BLAH, BLAH, BLAH, Mateo!" was all he ever heard anymore. He knew his parents wouldn't follow through on their threats; they never did. They always fed him, and even when they banished him to his room, he didn't care. In fact, he liked it. Alex would have been bored to tears and begged his parents to let him out, but Mateo enjoyed being alone. It was easier to fantasize when there were no distractions.

Mateo's teachers were likewise helpless in the face of his lack of ambition.

"If you do well in school this year," Mrs. Hatfield pointed out, "your parents said they'd take you to Disneyland."

This kind of promise would have thrilled most children, but Mateo didn't even blink an eye.

"I have my whole life to go to Disneyland," he answered (while twiddling with his pencil-sword). "I'm in no hurry."

"I wish he would have come with an owner's manual," his mother sighed one Saturday afternoon, a few weeks after Mateo's tenth birthday. "Instead, he came wrapped in a blue blanket with an encouraging smile from a nurse. Our coffee grinder came with more instructions!"

"It's so true, Evelyn," Mateo's father replied, heading out the door to the bank. He'd reluctantly agreed, once again, to send a 100 dollars to his younger brother Alonzo, and he wasn't happy about it. "Thank goodness we have nothing scheduled for Mateo today. I'm worn out from trying to make him cooperate."

Evelyn was a photographer and was working on a big project, so she disappeared into the family room with her camera and computer while Alex cycled over to a friend's house. Meanwhile, Mateo was upstairs in his bedroom, alone, and doing (you guessed it) nothing. In point-of-fact, he was lying on his bed, staring at the ceiling, and daydreaming that he was living on a star.

"I'd have to wear a fireproof suit, of course," he thought, "or I'd burn up."

And it was just then, as he was fashioning the special-order Kevlar suit in his mind, that he first saw *the crack*.

The Crack

It was an ordinary-looking crack that might have gone unnoticed by another boy. But children like Mateo spend many hours staring at their bedroom ceilings because they're so often sent to their rooms as punishment. Thus, they're intimately familiar with their ceilings and notice when something is amiss.

The crack was *new*, of that he was sure, and though he wasn't normally a curious boy (his vivid imagination kept him plenty busy), he found himself strangely drawn to it.

"If I stand on my bed and stretch *all* the way up," he thought, "I might be able to reach it."

And when he attempted this, like a moth drawn to a flame, the tips of his fingers tingled and turned a magnificent shade of light purple that closely resembled the color of the "Lush Lavender" crayon in his 64-color Kidz-Art Craft Set. His fingers hadn't quite reached the crack. He was too short for that. But his fingers changed color nonetheless, and it was obvious that the crack was responsible. What else could have caused it?

Many ten-year-olds faced with such an alarming situation might have screamed and raced off to tell their parents. But we must remember that Mateo had *Presence*. So instead, he just stared at his fingers, with great interest, and kept staring at them, waiting to see if they would turn back to their normal, buttery light brown.

Meanwhile, he noticed (and not for the first time) the funny shape that all hands have, and how you can't stack the left hand on top of the right hand and make them fit. This made for fun shadow play. Mateo made the "shadow thumb" of one hand joust with the "shadow hand" of the other, a game that might normally have kept him entertained all the way to dinner.

But as the minutes passed, and Mateo realized that the lavender color on his fingers was not going to vanish all by itself, he wandered into the kitchen. He was starving and ready for his eighth enormous snack of the day, and hunger was one of the few things that made Mateo snap to attention and take action.

As Mateo opened the refrigerator and considered its contents, it occurred to him that his mother would be very angry if he showed up to dinner with lavender fingers. She was picky about cleanliness, as well as a host of other things. She would likely accuse him of being up to some kind of mischief when he should have been doing something useful with his free time (like retirement planning). So Mateo decided that he would lie. He would lie because it was the easiest way to cover his tracks when he was being present instead of being productive. And with his rich imagination, Mateo could dream up some real whoppers.

"I'll say that Alex painted them while I was sleeping," he thought with a devilish grin. "That will get *me* off the hook and *him* into trouble!"

Now I want to assure you that Mateo was not a mean child; not at all. But his parents were always holding up Alex as a model for the kind of kid they wanted him to be, and it hurt his feelings.

"Why can't you be more like Alex? He doesn't muck around! Watch him at batting practice. Watch him whiz through his homework. Watch and learn!"

These comparisons made Mateo feel very small indeed, and we can't blame him for having revenge fantasies against Alex on a fairly regular basis: Alex failing out of second grade, Alex getting booted off the baseball team, Alex *in jail*. If a bully had tried to beat up Alex after school, though, Mateo would have rushed to his brother's aid. Down deep inside, where it mattered, Mateo loved him.

Fortunately, for it is never a good idea to tell a lie (you almost always get found out), Mateo discovered how to remove the lavender stain from his fingers. After attempting to wash it off with soap and water, ketchup, olive oil, orange juice, and Happy Cow Organic Meatless Beef-Flavored Barbeque Sauce (his parents were vegetarians and strictly enforced their diet on him), he finally discovered that soda worked. And when his mother came into the kitchen later and found all these items lying about (along with Mateo's unwashed silverware, which I'm sorry to report he left in the sink), she simply put them away without another thought.

After he was finished eating, Mateo was eager to get back to the crack and do some more exploring. If *almost* touching the crack had made his fingers tingle and turn lavender, what would happen if he actually *did* touch it?"

His fingers would turn lavender again (that much was obvious) but he knew how to remove the color now. And perhaps something much more spectacular would happen that would get him out of school the next day. This idea was appealing to Mateo because the Academic Awards Ceremony was scheduled for lunch time and all the kids would be getting a plaque of one kind or another, except him.

Mrs. Hatfield had told his mother at the last parent-teacher conference that she "simply couldn't justify" giving him an award, "even for participation." After hearing that, his mother had yanked him into the car and driven away from the school at high speed, almost hitting one of his classmates in the crosswalk. He'd gotten a lecture from his father that evening too, but, as usual, he'd blocked out the words.

"BLAH, BLAH, BLAH, Mateo. Why didn't _you_ get a _BLAH, BLAH, BLAH?_"

Mateo had to place his rarely used desk chair on the mattress to reach the crack, and it was a difficult maneuver. The chair rocked unsteadily and threatened to topple over as he climbed onto it. And it did fall over (three times to be exact), but Mateo was so drawn to the crack that he kept on trying. Finally, on his fourth attempt, he was successful. He actually touched the crack. And the moment he did, he felt a jolt of electricity shoot from his fingers through his body and out his toes before the room disappeared from view and he was somewhere else altogether.

I would be remiss to lead you into the next few minutes of Mateo's unusual day without advising you to bring along some peanut butter sandwiches and a sword, for Mateo had neither and would soon regret it. But you have been forewarned and can run off and get them now. Then perhaps you'll be willing to share them with Mateo when we all get to where we're going, in Chapter Two.

Chapter 2

WHAT HAPPENED NEXT

First off, I must apologize for the teaser about the sword. It's true that Mateo will wield one before this story is done, but he won't be doing it right away and it won't be the King Arthur's type found in most children's adventure stories. Sometimes writers get a little ahead of themselves, especially at the end of the first chapter of an exciting book.

As for the peanut butter sandwiches, Mateo's need for them will be rather immediate, but will also involve an important decision on your part. So hold onto them for now. If you like, you can draw them in the space below, dog-ear the page, and come back and pick them up later. Or, you can draw them out on a separate piece of paper and tuck the drawing into a secret place that only you know about, so you can pull it out when the time comes.

But let's return to Mateo. What happened to him next is difficult for me to describe because nothing remotely like it has ever happened to me. However, since I'm the narrator of this extraordinary tale and it's my job to explain it, I'll do my best.

The moment the violent jolt of electricity exited his toes, Mateo was sucked up through the crack, which opened just wide enough to let him through before snapping shut behind him.

For one brief (but creepy) moment, Mateo found himself crouching in the cramped crawl space between his bedroom ceiling and the roof, staring into the eyes of a resident rat. But it was a short-lived encounter, for suddenly, he was siphoned upward again, so fast that his body thinned and distorted into a long, flexible noodle, slender enough to thread through a small hole in the roof and into the blue sky beyond.

Up, up, up he went, soaring through layer after layer of Earth's atmosphere, the sky growing darker and darker with each passing second until it was blacker than black and exploded with millions of twinkling stars.

But the stars didn't twinkle for very long; they morphed into streaks. By then, you see, Mateo was traveling faster than the speed of light through a space-time tunnel that only a few brilliant physicists believe exists. And this, it turns out, was lucky for him, for outer space is a very inhospitable place and it's best to cross it as quickly as possible.

Mateo was chilled to the bone, for the space between stars is very, very cold. And he was suffocating too, from lack of air. But worst of all, the sudden change in air pressure forced the air in his lungs to expand and the water in his soft tissues to vaporize. (Divers experience something similar when they surface from the deep ocean too quickly; it's a condition called "the bends.")

No one wants to die as a bubbling ice cube gasping for air, so I'm pleased to tell you that Mateo was spared this fate. Instead, all he really suffered was a nasty sunburn from being exposed to ultraviolet light with no space suit for protection, and he arrived at his final destination unscathed and back to his normal human-boy shape again, standing upright and alert in the middle of a forest, surrounded by trees bearing purple fruit.

The forest was eerily quiet, and after his adventure through space, Mateo instinctively knew he was no longer on Earth. But while you and I might have been a little nervous, and maybe even scuffled our feet to make some noise to keep us company, Mateo just stood there for more than a minute, feeling, more than anything else, that he'd arrived *home*. If you've ever come back from a long vacation, even one that was lots of fun, and felt an overwhelming sense of peace and safety when you walked in your front door, you'll know how Mateo felt. It was odd and unexpected, but he'd never felt so good in his entire life.

Mateo tried to hold onto the feeling, but it slipped away, and soon he was examining himself to make sure he wasn't injured. He seemed okay; no bones were broken at least. But the lavender color on his fingers had returned with a vengeance. No amount of soda, he was sure, could get rid of it now. If he ever got back home, his mother would be furious. But maybe some good could come from it.

"Perhaps Mrs. Hatfield will kick me out of school!" he thought, in sudden delight. "She'll tell my parents that my purple fingers are distracting the other students and I'm suspended forever!"

It was a fun fantasy, and Mateo could have spent many hours enjoying it. But, in the otherworldly forest, there were more interesting opportunities. So he walked over to the nearest tree and climbed into its dark branches, wondering if the purple fruit tasted sweet and juicy, like oranges, or bitter and chewy, like the curly mustard greens his mother so often served for dinner.

As it turned out, it was neither. It tasted like stale bread.

"Oh well," he told himself, "a boy can't be picky when he's starving."

He dug in and finished off an entire fruit, which was about the size of a mango but without the large seed, and then swung about for a while, pretending he was a monkey.

"*A monkey?*" you might be asking. "Really?"

Well, I'm afraid so. But if you're tempted to scoff at Mateo at this point in the story, please don't write him off quite yet. Swinging from branch to branch in an alien forest is actually a lot of fun, especially when the limbs of the trees you're swinging in are close together like the bars on a jungle gym. Any self-respecting child on such an adventure would surely have climbed high in the forest canopy to get a view and find out more about where he was. But that idea never crossed Mateo's mind. Instead, he played monkey for the next four hours, which I shall skip over to save time, and it was nearly sunset before he realized that dinnertime was fast approaching and he'd likely have to eat another piece of tasteless purple fruit or waste away from hunger.

It didn't occur to Mateo that he might fix his *own* dinner, by scouting through the forest to find something edible and then cooking it up over a camp fire.

Dinners at the fine house by the sea appeared on the table as if by magic, and Mateo's parents had long ago given up on asking him to help. He had some nebulous idea that cooking was involved, with pots and pans and oil and such. But beyond that, he was completely clueless.

Mateo was coddled, you see. His parents thought they were doing him a favor, but they had made him helpless and dependent instead. And at the age of ten, when boys in other cultures hunt game with arrows and bring it home to feed their families, this made Mateo a rather pathetic creature, though he never thought about himself like that.

In truth, Mateo was nowhere close to starvation, and could have subsisted for many months on seafood at the beaches nearby, if he'd only gone exploring. But instead, he started to feel very sorry for himself, spinning a story that a forest that had felt so wonderfully home-like had unfairly betrayed him by failing to provide dinner at the expected hour.

You can decide at this point whether you want to give Mateo the peanut butter sandwiches you brought with you into this chapter. But I advise against it because someone else in this story will soon need them much more than well-fed Mateo, and you may prefer to give them to her instead.

With his tummy grumbling loudly (unless you gave him the sandwiches), Mateo sat on a branch, his bare legs hanging into empty space, and watched the sun go down. He didn't actually see it set, of course, as he still hadn't bothered to climb high enough in the trees to do so. If he had, he would have seen the sun disappear into a beautiful tropical ocean, shaded by puffy clouds tinged with gold. But Mateo knew it was setting anyway because the sky mellowed into a soft blue-grey, which eventually faded to midnight blue, and stars began flickering to life where the once-bright sky had been.

Within half an hour, Mateo could see dozens of stars, shining like the fires of a distantly encamped army, spread at uneven distances among unseen hills and valleys. It was a vast army, Mateo decided, one that carried horse-loads of delicious, piping-hot food for the sharing. But try as he might, the imagined food just wasn't the same as real food, and his tummy rumbled and complained louder than ever (unless, of course, you gave him the sandwiches).

Mateo didn't know the names of the constellations at home and couldn't point out anything but the Big Dipper on a good night. So he didn't realize that the patterns of the stars above him were completely new. What he did notice, however, and with some confusion, was that as soon as the sky was quite dark, it began to get light again, as if the sun was coming back up after merely dipping below the horizon.

An eerie kind of twilight gradually took the stars away as he sat there, staring at the sky and fantasizing about food. The constellation that had looked vaguely like a pile of steaming spaghetti topped with a blob of delicious butter, blinked out. The circle of stars that was shaped like a pizza, faded away. And in the east…well, what was in the east requires several paragraphs to describe.

Not even hungry Mateo could imagine what was rising above the trees in the east looked anything like food. At first, he thought he was having double vision and he closed his eyes for a moment to clear them. But when he reopened them, the apparition was still there: two full moons peeking through the tangled branches of the trees. The first was very large, at least twice the size of Earth's moon, and much brighter. The second was about the size of Earth's moon, but dimmer, and pale orange.

Perhaps you've had the profoundly uneasy feeling that Mateo now experienced as he sat, awestruck, watching the moons make their grand entrance. His overwhelming urge was to hide—like a panicked mouse in the shade of a hawk's wing—and he threw his arms around the nearest branch and burrowed his head into the leaves. But the brightness of the moons-light (for *moons*-light it was) penetrated through his tightly puckered eyelids and even Mateo, with his well-developed skill for disappearing inside his imagination, could not escape.

Quick as lightning, he slid down the tree and began running as fast as he could, away from the moons, his moons-shadow leaping out in front of him as he ran.

The moons-light was so bright that he had no trouble seeing where he was going, and he was so athletic and quick that it took him almost no time to find a safer spot. Leaping over tree roots and downed branches, running for his life, eyes and mouth wide open with fright, he flew across the forest until he reached a meadow surrounded by granite boulders the size of houses. It was here, in the searing light of the two moons, that he spied a cave and, almost at the same instant, used his best baseball sliding moves to skid through the opening.

Mateo's heart was beating so wildly that he could feel the blood pounding inside his skull. His mouth went bone dry. For the first time that day, despite the warm and fuzzy feeling he'd had when he'd first arrived, he felt utter terror. If you've ever gotten lost from your parents in a strange city and had no idea where they were or how to get home, just multiply that feeling by 10 and you'll have a notion of how Mateo felt. Alone, or so he thought, he huddled in a tight ball, bringing his knees up close to his chest until they hurt. How long he sat like that is anyone's guess, but both moons were well above the veil of trees, their light extinguishing all the stars, by the time he began to relax again.

The entrance to the cave was very small (hence the need for the masterful baseball slide). But inside, it was large enough to stand up and move around. Moons-light poured through the opening and still alarmed and unsettled him, but he felt less fear now and he suspected that he might have overreacted. If you're in a different world, after a trip through space, there is no reason to expect there to be only one moon or that the moon(s) would be the same size as Earth's. In fact, the whole notion of being scared suddenly seemed rather silly to him and he was able to stand, a little shakily, and take a renewed interest in where he was.

Chapter 3

WHERE MATEO WAS

Where Mateo was is best described from the perspective of the other occupant of the cave, to whom Mateo will be introduced soon. From her vantage point, deep in the interior, it was a place where people go to find their children. This may seem very odd to you, because in our world parents keep close tabs on their offspring, especially these days, and don't need to go looking for them in caves.

But in her world, some children—*unseen* earth children—are not born in the normal way, by sex and pregnancy and childbirth classes. Instead, they're *found*, and not by parents who will raise the child together, but by a single person who has earned that privilege.

On Earth, it's difficult to raise a child all by yourself (just ask someone who's done it). But on the strange planet where Mateo found himself, unseen children don't arrive as infants. They arrive between the ages of seven and 12, so they're already partway raised and much of the hard work—like changing diapers and preventing them from toddling into pools and drowning—is already done. Moreover, the purpose of finding unseen children isn't to raise them to adults, who in turn will have their own children and do the same. Instead, it's to help them appreciate their natural gifts, the gifts their earth parents don't see, and put them to their most noble and powerful use. It usually takes several months and, if all goes well, the child is returned to earth and then it's time to find another unseen child and start the process all over again.

To master the skills required to find and train a child, a man or woman must attend an elite school called an academy. While there, they "stripe" in a gift, which is like majoring in a subject in college. There are many different kinds of stripes to earn, and some students earn more than one. But the important thing is that when they graduate, they're eligible to find children whose gifts match their stripes. For example, a graduate who earned a stripe in *Forging New Paths* is allowed to find a child who has that gift. But this same person wouldn't be allowed to find a child with the gift of *Telling Tall Tales*. That child would belong to another.

The woman in the cave had earned two stripes during her years at the academy, *Presence* and *Ignoring Rules*, and she'd found four children thus far and trained them all successfully. But her last two attempts to find a child had been very disappointing. A child had failed to appear, so she'd gone home to her cave on Cairntip Island, several hundred miles away, empty-handed. This time, she was hoping to have better luck.

A few weeks before, she, and several others like her, had been dropped off on Finding Island, which is covered with the kind of purple-fruited trees that Mateo had explored earlier that day. She had separated herself from the group and been alone ever since, wandering from one cave to another trying to find a comfortable spot to hunker down and wait.

Several earlier caves had proved damp and uncomfortable. One had even given her a nasty rash. This cave, with its tiny opening and dry internal climate, was decidedly to her liking, so she set up camp along one end, using a conveniently located fissure to serve as a smoke hole for her cooking fire. It was here that she'd spent her days eating the tasteless purple Finding Fruit and sleeping through the nights dreaming of unseen children.

By the time Mateo arrived, the moons, Lunera and Ru, had passed through many different phases, and the woman was getting sick and tired of eating the Finding Fruit. It was the only food she was permitted to eat during a "finding" and there were only so many recipes for serving up the stuff. She'd run through them in the first two weeks. It was nutritious and wildly popular in health food stores back on Cairntip. But for people like her, who had to subsist on it for long periods, its purple flesh had no allure. She'd begged and prayed for her child to appear, if only to break the tasteless tedium she was enduring. Yet day after day passed with no "findling" and no end of the Finding Fruit.

I will give you this opportunity to be grateful you didn't give your peanut butter sandwiches to Mateo (unless you did, of course), as this poor creature is clearly far more desperate for food than he was. So if you saved the sandwiches, continue on to the next few paragraphs. If you didn't, you can skip them, though my guess is that you'll be tempted to peek anyway to see what would have happened if you had.

One late afternoon, after yet another lunch of Finding Fruit fritters, the woman was gathering firewood when she came across a delightful surprise: three peanut butter sandwiches all tied up in waxed paper and string.

"It must be an apparition!" she cried with joy as she set upon them. She knew she was breaking the rules, but it seemed like fate that they'd crossed her path so unexpectedly. So, sitting on a log in a sliver of dust-laden light that slanted through the wide branches overhead, she savored every bite, astonished at her good luck, barely daring to wonder where they'd come from lest they disappear.

It was one of the high points of her life, and one she would always remember with deep joy and gratitude: the day on the log in the Finding Forest with the peanut butter from the sandwiches sticking to the roof of her mouth. Yum.

And well done for saving your sandwiches for her!

And now, we return to the cave, where the woman lay asleep, dreaming of earth children. In this particular dream, the child was a boy with bright red hair, with the gift of *Fearlessness*. In other dreams, it had been a Japanese boy with a wicked smile who had the gift of *Humor*; a freckled-faced girl with soft blue eyes who *Cared about Animals*; a heavy-set boy from Zanzibar who *Slept Soundly*. Each child, in turn, had marched through her nightly visions, drawn her in, and then released her. For they were not *her* child; they didn't have the gifts that matched her stripes. As the woman slept, the red-haired boy did a dream-dance, recklessly stomping over her frontal cortex (fearless children can be very destructive until they've been properly trained), and she tossed and turned. But she would have sat bolt upright if she'd known that her findling was running headlong through the Finding Forest toward her that very moment, and was seconds away from making his noisy entrance.

CULLUMP! CRASH! CRASH! And then **"Ouch!"** were the sounds that rung through the cave as Mateo dove through the entrance to escape the terrifying moons-light.

The woman woke with a start, as people do when a loud noise interrupts them in deep sleep, and she gave an involuntary gasp. In the past, her findlings had arrived gently and romantically. One was dropped in her lap by a passing red-beaked gull, while another floated into her camp on a westerly breeze. She'd heard stories of sudden arrivals, but not one as jolting and dramatic as this. Perhaps this was not her child at all, but one of her colleagues who'd gone insane eating Finding Fruit and was murderous for flesh as she herself had been on several recent occasions, though she never would have acted on it. Or perhaps this was just another dream—this time a nightmare—sent to test her patience and forbearance, sent to torture her for one more night with the promise of a child. The woman didn't know what to do, but as she shrunk from her bed and cowered against the walls of the cave, eyes wide with a mixture of fear and hope, she saw that the intruder did appear to be a child, and very afraid.

Another person might have instantly gone to comfort Mateo. But the woman was undecided and chose to wait. Or, rather, her indecisiveness prevented her from making a decision (as she was honest to point out when she recounted the story later), and as the minutes passed and the child remained curled up in a ball, shaking and clearly miserable, she simply sat, or stood and slapped her hands gently on her legs to make sure she wasn't dreaming. You see, she fiercely wanted the child to be her findling, and was terrified of being disappointed. It was as if she'd woken up on Christmas morning, her stomach fluttering because she hoped that one of the brightly wrapped presents under the Christmas tree contained the gift she *really* wanted, but was so afraid it might not, that she was paralyzed. It was rather cowardly on her part to delay the possible pain, but understandable.

Finally, though, as the last vestiges of the evening's Finding Fruit stew made their complete passage through her reluctant belly, the child stood up. And oh! He was so clearly an Earth child, solidly built, with lean muscles and flawless skin, and just the right age for a findling. But his real beauty was in his big brown eyes, which shone, unblinking, like two steady lanterns in his tear-streaked face when he turned to look at her.

And then she knew. The eyes told her. Her child, her findling, had arrived: a boy with the gift of *Presence*. And at the most auspicious time for a finding—at a harvest syzygy, when Lunera and Ru were both full, the night skies were almost as bright as day, the ocean pulled far away from the land at low tide, and there were shellfish and crabs for the taking.

It seemed too good to be true but there was no doubt, no doubt at all.

So when the child looked directly at her and asked in a whisper, "Who are you?" she felt no further hesitation.

"I'm Ideth," she replied. "And I'm your uppy."

Chapter 4

FIVE THINGS YOU NEED TO KNOW

Now that Mateo and his uppy have been united, we're going to give them some time to get to know each other. Mateo needs to know his uppy's story and she needs to know his. We already know both, or at least the gist of what they're going to share with one another right now. There's no point listening in on the conversation, especially since we have some important matters to cover in the meantime. So we're going to take a break in Mateo's story and I'm going to tell you five things you need to know about Ideth's planet and the people who live there. Then, in Chapter Five, we'll see what's happening back in Monterey, where Mateo has gone mysteriously missing.

#1: Where on Earth is Urth?

You probably already know that Earth isn't the only planet in the Universe. In fact, our sun is only one of about 100 sextillion stars. Not all of the stars have planets like Earth, of course, where life is possible. But billions do. And Ideth's world is one of them, 64,000 light years away, in the *Obscured Arm* of our galaxy, the Milky Way. You can't see the stars in that arm when you look into the sky, even high up in the mountains on a very dark night, because they're so far away and the core of our galaxy blocks the view. But it exists all right, and lots of interesting happenings go on over there.

As you may know, 64,000 light years is a long, long way. In fact, it's 376,231,907,486,592,300 miles, which means that if you drove your parents' car at 70 miles an hour all day and all night, it would take you about 613 billion years to get there. My guess is that your parents wouldn't be willing to loan you their car for such a trip and, anyway, you'd be dead of old age before you got as far as Jupiter. How unseen children complete the journey in barely the blink of an eye is something quite mysterious. But I won't call it magic because most of the things we call magic don't turn out to be magic at all, but simply things we don't understand yet. And when we understand them, we no longer call them magic.

The name of Ideth's planet is spelled U-R-T-H, which (confusingly) is pronounced just like "Earth." Since the names are spelled differently, though, reading this book to yourself won't be confusing; you'll always know which is which. But reading it aloud to someone else would likely perplex them. So, if you like, you can pronounce the planet "yurth." After all, it's unlikely that you'll ever be reading this book to a native urthling (who might be offended and try to correct you), and I promise never to tell.

You might think a planet on the other side of our galaxy would be very different from Earth. It might be much larger, for example, and made mostly of light gases, like Jupiter and Saturn. Or it might be small, like Mercury, with almost no atmosphere at all and so close to a star that if you landed there you'd burn up right away (unless you had a special-order Kevlar suit). But Urth is very similar to Earth. In fact, urthlings call Earth a "sister planet." Thus, when you're reading this story and your imagination begins to paint pictures, assume that Urth and Earth are much the same, except where I point out the differences.

#2. Urth's Tides and Syzygies

As you already know, Urth has two moons. When you're visiting such a planet, it's helpful to know something about ocean tides. You may have learned in school (I certainly hope you have) that our moon's pull on the earth causes our tides. The sun plays a role, too, though it is farther away and its effect on our tides is therefore weaker. There are interesting equations that govern the behavior of tides, and if you are lucky enough to have the gift of *Loving Numbers*, you might want to look them up on the internet for fun. Most of us don't think that would be fun at all, and fortunately we don't need the equations to describe what happens, because it's almost as wonderful without them.

Now I want to point out, before we get any further into tides, that many children (not to mention adults) are likely to find the next few paragraphs rather confusing. But I hope you'll stick in there and read them anyway, making drawings in the margins if you like, for it's all very interesting, too.

When you visit the ocean, you can usually find a tide table somewhere, either in the hotel where you're staying or in one of the shops where your parents like to hang about and look at stuff while you're bored and anxious to play on the beach. What you'll notice from the tables is that the tide is high twice a day and low twice a day. But sometimes the high tides are really high and the low tides are really low. It's fun to go down to the beach when the tides are extreme like that. When the tide goes *way out*, you have much more beach to build sand castles on, and when the tide comes *way in*, there is barely any beach left at all.

What you probably don't know (and kudos to you if you do) is that the most extreme tides take place when the moon, earth, and sun are all positioned in a straight line. This only happens when our moon is in its "new" or "full" phases. The other concept to understand is that a full moon is up all night because it's opposite the sun, with earth in the middle. Thus, it rises at sunset and sets at sunrise. New moons, by contrast, appear (at least from earth) to be right near the sun and follow it very closely. They rise at sunrise and set at sunset, just like the sun.

Some people think the moon is only up at night, which is very silly. If you look for it, in case you haven't already, it's most noticeable at first quarter ("half moon"). A first quarter moon rises around noon and sets around midnight, so it's easy to spot in the mid-afternoon, if you just look up. Of course, some people (like Mateo's parents) are so busy that they rarely bother, which is sad because the moon is quite beautiful and translucent when it's framed by a bright blue sky.

The least extreme tides occur when the sun and moon are pulling on earth in different directions. During these so-called "neap tides," there's always some beach to play on, and if you build your sandcastles reasonably far from the surf, they might last for a few days (unless some mean kid comes and knocks them down).

The same general rules about tides apply on Urth, but there are two moons buzzing about and the effects of this are quite startling, at least to strangers. Usually, the pulls of the moons and sun counteract each other so the tides don't vary too much. But, when everything lines up just right, the tides are extreme indeed. And because there are two moons, there aren't just two ways this can happen; there are four: when both moons are full; when both moons are new; when the first moon is full and the second moon is new; or when the first moon is new and the second moon is full. These events are called *syzygies* (SIZZ-UH-GEEZ) and are going to be very important in this story.

Trilogies, a term you'll also encounter, are syzygies when both moons are new (the sun and both moons are on the same side of urth). During a trilogy, the nights are very dark, and all the stars come out. For urthlings (unlike us), this is a rare sight and a cause for celebration, much like a lunar eclipse on Earth, when city folk drive out into the countryside to get a better view.

Again, I hope you don't fret too much if you're confused about the tides; you needn't bother about the details. The Head Astronomer at the Ilck Observatory on Cairntip, Dr. Smusare

Fiddle, has his hands full tracking Lunera, Ru and their resultant tides, syzygies, trilogies, and eclipses. If you ever meet him, he'll be happy (ecstatic in fact) to show you his complicated diagrams, labeled up with befuddling words like *celestial equator,* *perihelion, aphelion, perigee,* and *apogee.* For reading this book, though, you mainly need to keep in mind that urth tides are very complex and can be much more extreme than what you're used to on our planet.

#3. Urth Years and Renaming

Urth travels around its sun twice as fast as Earth does, so urth years (UY) are half as long as earth years (EY). This means that if you're 10 years old (EY), you're about 20 years old (UY). Think about it: urthlings get twice as many birthdays as we do! But they don't celebrate them in the same way. Instead, they celebrate "renamings," which (in my opinion) are far more interesting.

Every urthling is given a name at birth (like Bart, Robert, Lucia, or Patti). But when they are about 16 UY (remember to divide by two to convert to EY), they rename themselves. This is a long-standing urth tradition and an important part of growing up. Before they rename, children are expected to obey their parents, without question. But after their Renaming Ceremony (an elaborate affair), they are given much more freedom than before. They can break rules from time to time without getting into trouble, and are even able to make up their own rules, like having breakfast at dinnertime so they can get more pancakes or choosing to sleep outside in a tent rather than in their regular bed.

Renaming, though, cannot be done willy-nilly. For example, a boy with the unfortunate name of Muffin can't rename himself John. Instead, he is limited to the same letters that are in his original name. But he shuffles them around to create an anagram of "Muffin" that he likes better. For example, he could rename himself Niffum or Iffnum (which, I think you'll agree, are both a great improvement over Muffin). Similarly, Bart might become Brat or (far better) Tarb, and Patti might become Attip, Tipat, or Patit. This explains why Ideth has such an odd name. She was born Edith, but when she was 19 (UY), she renamed herself, announcing to her parents that she planned to go to bed whenever she liked and there was nothing they could do about it.

Soon after an unseen child is found by his uppy, he has to rename himself, too. Since you're going to be spending quite a bit of time on Urth as you read this book, you might want to anagram your own name, just for fun. If you're lucky enough to have a long name, like Constantine or Anastasia, I congratulate you. Children with fortunate names like that have dozens of renames to choose from, and writing out all the possibilities can take hours.

#4. Urthlings are Islanders

Urth used to have six big continents and four oceans. Much like our planet, there were coastlines, flat plains, and mountain ranges that rose thousands of feet into the sky. But then, many generations before Ideth was born, the ice caps at the poles began to shrink unexpectedly, wearing away year by year until there was almost no ice left.

This "great melt" (as it's called by urthlings) raised the ocean levels and reduced the planet to a few dozen islands. Plants and animals that flourished in dry climates or high altitudes disappeared in the space of only a few decades, and urthlings, who made their living from the sea, had to relocate inland to where the tips of the mountains had once been, to keep their heads above water.

The largest of urth's islands (and Ideth's home) was once the summit of a great mountain twice the height of our Mount Kilimanjaro, thronged by mighty glaciers, but it was cut down to only a few hundred feet in the great melt. The other islands are smaller and huddle in clusters, the remnants of old mountain ranges. Uppies always find their children on Finding Island, but quickly ferry them to training islands appropriate for their gifts. Some uppies have to travel weeks to get their findlings properly situated, while others only have to travel a few hours. But whatever the destination, it's always an island of one sort or another. There's no other choice.

#5. What Urthlings Look Like and Why

Because urthlings live on the coast and spend a lot of time in the water, their bodies have some of the same features as marine mammals on our planet. For example, they can "see" underwater by emitting pulses of sound, which makes it possible for them to navigate when the ocean is murky or especially

deep. Their feet are slightly webbed too, to aid in swimming (which they call "paddling"), and they have a layer of shimmering indigo blubber around their midsections to keep them buoyant and warm in chilly water. However, urthlings have two peculiarities that aren't seen in any animals on Earth: the hair on their heads is bushy and long, which gives young children something to hang onto when they are paddling alongside their parents, and they have lavender skin, which I can't really explain. Nor can I explain why the fingers of earth children turn lavender when they arrive on Urth, but, as you know, they do.

There are many excellent and anatomically correct drawings of urthlings in a book called *A Traveler's Guide to Urth*, and I strongly suggest that you purchase, rent, borrow, or steal a copy if you can find one. They're hard to come by. I found mine in a dusty little bookstore in Reykjavik, Iceland. I have no idea how it got there, but I'll bet it's an interesting tale.

So there you go. I've wrapped up everything you need to know about Urth and urthlings in one chapter so you've got your footing. In fact, you now know more about Urth than Mateo does. But he'll learn as his adventure unfolds, so you needn't fret about him unless you have the gift of *Worrying*, in which case you won't be able to help yourself.

Chapter 5

WHAT'S BEEN HAPPENING
IN MONTEREY

There is nothing more painful for a parent than losing a child. Imagine that you have a favorite pet (and if you do, this mental exercise will be easier) and one day it simply disappeared. If it was a dog, perhaps you left him in the yard, and when you came home, he was no longer there. Or if it was a goldfish, you walked into the living room and found her fishbowl empty. In addition to the profound feeling of loss, you would also feel responsible, because caring for the pet was your job and you failed to protect it. There's also the *not knowing what happened*, which can be even worse and might eat you alive inside.

Are you imagining how you would feel? Now multiply that feeling by a thousand times, and then multiply that new feeling by another thousand times and you'll know how Mateo's parents felt when he didn't show up for dinner, a meal that he had never missed in his life.

At first, his parents were annoyed. *Where was he? Had he lost track of time? Had he arranged to eat dinner at a friend's house and forgotten to call and tell them?*

Then they got angry. *What the heck was the kid doing? What game was he playing? How could he do this to us?*

But as time passed, their anger slowly turned to concern, their concern turned to fear, and their fear turned into the feeling you just finished trying to imagine.

They called the parents of all his friends. They went through their fine house, checking under every bed, in every bathtub, and in every closet. They went out into the yard and called his name. They peered fearfully into their swimming pool and went up and down the block, in both directions, frantically screaming "Mateo! Mateo!" Finally, they called the police. By nine that evening, a police helicopter was in the air, scanning the neighborhood and nearby beaches with a bright spotlight. By 11, the television news crews had arrived.

Evelyn clutched her cell phone, afraid to put it down for even a single instant in case Mateo called. His father, Roberto, spoke to the news crews and gave them a recent photo of Mateo for broadcast. Alex (who, if you remember, is Mateo's younger brother) was so terrified that he refused to go and stay with a neighbor and crouched, frozen with fear, in the kitchen next to his mother, his hands gripping her arm.

As the hours passed, the house filled with police officers, who questioned everyone and took Mateo's toothbrush for DNA.

"If his body is ever found," one of the cops said unfeelingly, "the DNA on this toothbrush will allow us to identify it. Sometimes we only find body parts, you see, or skeletons. DNA is very helpful in such instances."

This comment made Evelyn's heart drop and Roberto's hair stand on end. *If his body is ever found.* Did the cops already think that Mateo was dead?

The police went through the house from top to bottom, gathering additional photos of Mateo off Evelyn's computer: Mateo playing baseball, Mateo at a friend's birthday party eating pizza, Mateo grinning and standing with friends at summer camp, Mateo twiddling a pencil. They interviewed his parents again and again.

"When did you last see him? What was he wearing? Was he upset about anything? Who are his friends and where do they live? Has he ever disappeared like this before?"

To each question, his family gave their best answers.

"I was the one who last saw him, I think," Evelyn said, choking down tears, "when I sent him to his bedroom for dawdling over his homework. He was wearing a pair of black shorts and a red t-shirt. He had socks on, I think, but no shoes."

"He's a bit of a loner," Roberto added. "He only has a few good friends. But here's a list of the boys on his baseball team. Here's a list of his school buddies. And no, no, no—he has *never* disappeared like this before. He's never even skipped a meal!"

Most missing children are found within 24 hours of their disappearance, so as friends and family members began arriving in Monterey the next morning, eager to help, they all offered comforting words.

"Don't worry, he'll show up soon. They're bound to find him. The cops know what they're doing."

Mateo's grandmother even said, "Goodness, we'll all be laughing about this by the same time tomorrow," which was received very coldly, but excused because she was elderly and "not quite all there" (if you know what I mean).

Alex was especially hard hit. He was a gregarious but sensitive child, and the sudden loss of his brother left him heartsick. But he had the gift of *Getting Things Done* and doers desperately need to be busy, so his mind raced this way and that trying to think of something.

"We need to put up flyers!" he shouted, suddenly inspired. "That's what they do on TV when a child is missing!"

Alex fled back to his bedroom to start making one. His flyer wasn't perfect and Evelyn (who had the gift of *Looking Closely*) found a couple of spelling errors and corrected them with a red pen. It was otherwise nicely crafted, though, and a few hours later, dozens of people were scattering into different areas of Monterey and nearby towns with masking tape and pushpins in hand.

"MISSING BOY" was emblazoned across the top of the flyer, followed by Alex's description of his brother and a photograph of Mateo in his baseball uniform. There was also the promise of a $50,000 reward.

Mateo's father had phoned every member of his large Italian family, including Uncle Alonzo, to ask for donations. He was sure that by the time someone called with a lead, which he desperately prayed they would soon, he'd be able to pony up the money. He had to.

The fact that Evelyn was a professional photographer and had taken literally thousands of photographs of her ne'er-do-well son, was a definite plus. The media was saturated with photographs of Mateo. Channel 12 broadcast a very impressive photo of him deftly sliding into first base. There were videos of Mateo as well. The most recent was shot at his tenth birthday party, where he rolled his eyes, made funny faces, and (unfortunately) appeared like a silly, spoiled little boy who was of questionable value to anyone other than his distraught parents.

The head of the Missing Children's Task Force, an organization that offered assistance to families in the early stages of a possible abduction case, stopped by around noon. Two well-meaning, businesslike women came to the house to advise Mateo's parents about setting up a volunteer center to coordinate a search independent of the police investigation.

One of them turned a pair of pitying eyes on Evelyn and said, "You know, dear, the police have *no idea* what they're doing. Why our David has been missing for more than two years and they haven't turned up a single lead."

This wasn't what Mateo's mother had hoped to hear, of course, but at least the women were going to help them find Mateo and for that she was grateful.

There were also calls from two psychics. The first provided a vague description of Mateo's location as "near a lake or large body of water, with some kind of greenery, and perhaps a culvert." She then whipped off an e-mail with an attachment that detailed her retainer agreement: "$10,000 down. $5,000 non-refundable; $5,000 refundable if the missing child is not recovered within one year."

"One *year*!" thought Mateo's mother in horror. "These people are thieves!"

The second psychic offered up her services "free to grieving souls" and then delivered the crushing blow: "He's dead, poor thing. But I guess you probably already suspected that."

Mateo's parents were exhausted but unable to sleep. Evelyn was led to a back bedroom by a friend and made to lie down, "even if it's just for a few minutes, honey."

But it was no use. Even as Evelyn's eyes closed, her heart was hammering, her stomach was cramping from anxiety, and her mind was racing from one "What if?" scenario to another, searching desperately for hope in any corner where it might be hiding.

"Oh, please, please, *PLEASE*," she gasped, squeezing her eyes shut and rolling into a fetal position, a pillow between her knees. Alex brought her a cup of tea, but she couldn't drink it.

As more hours passed with no news, the volunteers began to return to their own homes for dinner, and the fine house by the sea became quiet. Mateo's parents crawled into bed beside one another, lost in an agony that only the two of them could truly understand. Evelyn looked at the clock on the nightstand. It was 11:55 PM.

"Nearly midnight," she whispered to Roberto with overwhelming dread. "It's been more than 24 hours. Missing

children are usually found within 24 hours. Oh please let him still be alive. I love him so!"

There was a shuffle from the doorway as Mateo's grandmother made her way back to bed after a trip to the bathroom.

"You know," she said with a little chuckle, popping her head into the bedroom, "we'll all be laughing about this the same time next week!"

Then she hobbled on down the hallway, thinking she'd said something helpful and uplifting when, in fact, her words hung like doom in the air.

Chapter 6

UPPY SURFING
AND DUCKY SACKS

When someone goes missing, especially if that person is having a mind-bending adventure on the other side of the galaxy, it is much, much better to be the one missing than the one left behind. In truth, Mateo hadn't given a moment's thought to what might be happening back home in Monterey.

Who can blame him? He'd been sucked through a crack in his bedroom ceiling, flung 64,000 light years across the vacuum of space, survived the shock of the terrifying moonslight, and had met Ideth, his uppy, a very odd-looking woman who seemed delighted to have run into him.

Ideth was only an inch or two taller than Mateo and had the wrinkles and demeanor of his grandmother. She could be as old as 60 he guessed, though he was a very poor judge of age and might have been 20 years off either way. She puttered about like his grandmother too, a pair of glasses perched on her head and another hanging around her neck by a chain. Her lavender skin was no surprise, but her webbed feet were so strange that Mateo had a hard time keeping his eyes off them. She also wore a weird outfit that made her look like she was about to compete in a triathlon. Her shimmering dark purple swimsuit (or so it seemed to him) covered her entire body except her arms, legs, and head. In truth, she looked to Mateo like a cross between a human being, a duck, and a seal, and it was all he could do to smother his giggles.

"So you see, Mateo," Ideth said, having just explained to him some of what I told you about in Chapter Four, "we won't stay on Finding Island for very long. You belong on Krog Pad and it will be such a relief to get moving. I don't think I can stand more than one more day of Finding Fruit. I can almost taste fresh lobster with Amdar Pot-Nut butter and oysters fresh from the shell!"

It was the fourth time Ideth had mentioned food and Mateo began to think she was rather obsessed by it. (Obsessions are always much easier to identify in others than in yourself.) But he didn't mind. He loved the way she hovered about him, as if he was a little prince, attending to his every need. She paid rapt attention to what he said and appeared completely smitten by him. It was the first time that Mateo could ever remember being treated like that and it felt so good that he opened right up and told Ideth all kinds of truths he'd never told his parents, like the fact that he sometimes discarded his homework in the dumpster by the school library on his way home, which made her laugh and seem to admire him all the more.

For her part, Ideth was paddling on air. After her two recent failures, she had finally found a child again. He had *Presence*, too, which was the favorite of her two stripes. Training children who *Ignored Rules* could be quite an ordeal, as her second finding had taught her in no uncertain terms. Yoko hadn't cooperated with anything and it had taken almost a year to complete her training and return her back home to Tokyo, where her parents thought she'd drowned in a lake and were delighted to learn that she was still alive.

But this finding would be different! She would take Mateo to Krog Pad Island as soon as she'd sent up her flare the next morning. Laup, the boatman, would be watching for it and would bring them supplies for their paddle to Krog Pad, including delicious foods she hadn't tasted in weeks.

Meanwhile, Mateo was wondering if Ideth was a triathlete, impressed at the thought that he might have landed among a race of super-athletes who could do all kinds of amazing things. Hey! Maybe they could train him to be a super athlete too, and when he got back to Monterey he would go to the Olympics. His parents would then forget all about Alex and brag about *him* (for once) to all their friends. He could see himself, on the Olympic podium, with 10 gold medals hanging around his ennobled neck, waving to the crowd and the cameras, flooded in light, the center of everyone's attention. When he got back to school, all his friends would whisper in the halls when he passed: "There he goes, *MATEO MARINO*. He's back from the Olympics with 10 gold medals! No one's ever won 10 gold medals in uppy surfing!"

Mateo smiled as his fantasy came to its lofty end. And when he opened his eyes (for he'd closed them to help himself imagine), he saw that Ideth was smiling too.

"That was a *wonderful* fantasy, Mateo!" she said, clapping her hands. "There's no such thing as uppy surfing, but the idea is simply delightful. Am I right, or am I right?" She was clearly charmed.

Mateo's chest swelled with pleasure, but then he became alarmed.

"How did you know about my fantasy?" he asked, a little off balance. He wasn't sure he liked the idea of someone eavesdropping on his imagination, which had always been his private refuge. But at the same time, he was proud. In Monterey, he spent most of his homework hour (which typically expanded into three or four hours of evading his parents' frustrated glares, exasperated sighs, and "helpful" suggestions) galloping through acres of unexplored dreamland, only to pay for it later ("BLAH, BLAH, BLAH, Mateo!"). Yet Ideth seemed to like his imagination.

"Oh, you won't have any secrets from me while you're here," she said. "I understriped in *Mind Reading* at the uppy academy, and I'm quite skilled at it."

She thought back to her academy days with pleasure; she'd been so happy there.

"Anyway, right now, I need to feed you and prepare a nice soft place for you to sleep. I brought enough supplies for two, of course, hoping you'd show. And you're quite hungry and tired now. You must be."

Mateo suddenly felt exhausted, almost as if Ideth's words had put a spell on him, and the hunger pains came back to his consciousness with full force.

"Unfortunately," she was saying, "it will be Finding Fruit pudding this time. But the bedding is made of the best Cairntip Doow Duck down, and once you burrow into that, I won't be seeing you awake any time soon, moons-light or no!"

The pudding turned out to be only slightly better than the bland fruit itself, and as Mateo nibbled at it, he dreamed of pancakes slathered with butter and maple syrup.

"Nice fantasy!" Ideth praised him with relish. "I can almost smell the butter now! Am I right or am I right?"

They ate the pudding off two delicate plates in the circle of light thrown by Ideth's hurricane lamp, which cast huge shadows against the walls of the cave. The moons-light was much gentler now that the moons were lower in the sky and the opening of the cave had been cast into shade. By the time they were done eating and Ideth had rinsed and stacked the dishes, Mateo was grateful to crawl into his "ducky-sack" (as Ideth called it). Then Ideth settled into her own and they were side-by-side in the almost-dark.

"It's not a swimsuit," Ideth whispered before they both fell asleep. "I never bring along clothes on a finding. Too much fuss for me, though other uppies bring along whole trunks of needless stuff. You see, we have this layer of indigo blubber around our midsection to keep us warm and buoyant in the sea. I know it looks like a swimsuit to you, but we can't take it off."

"Mom hates the layer of fat around her belly and is always complaining about it," Mateo replied.

"Well that's just silly," Ideth said, as she yawned and turned over on her side. "The more blubber the better, I say."

After that, they both fell quiet and drifted off to sleep, cradled in the darkness of the cave and the comfort of each other.

It was a very sweet scene: the gently snoring uppy and her newly found findling, both cuddled up in their ducky sacks, all warm and toasty. And while Mateo was so tired that he entered a dreamless sleep beyond exhaustion, Ideth's mind was filled with dreams of the future and planning for the marvelous days that lay ahead.

Chapter 7

OUT TO THE BEACH

Ideth was awake and puttering as soon as the first rays of sunlight filtered into the cave. She'd fashioned a broom from tree branches and was sweeping: *Scrape, scrape, scrape, scrape, scrape, scrape.* Then she started moving pots about: *Bang, clatter, "oops!" clatter, BANG, "Darn it!"*

A fire was next, and after several attempts, it flamed to life. Then there was crackling and popping and Ideth left the cave briefly, returning with a pot of water: *swing, swing, slush, slush.*

All of this was done with a kind of hush-hush, as if Ideth was trying very hard not to wake up Mateo. But it was no good. Mateo came to consciousness as the muted noises continued, and became more and more annoyed as he dropped off to sleep one moment, only to be awakened the next. For a boy who prefers to sleep until noon, it was a bit much. Ideth's obvious attempts *not* to wake him only made her behavior more annoying, and after a few minutes he gave up and decided it was better to wake up altogether. Besides, what was that smell coming from the pot Ideth was heating over the fire?

"Finding Fruit oatmeal," she said, as she saw him look up and sniff. "And this is the last day of it, thank goodness!"

Mateo had been dreaming of an extra-large Go Vegan fast food black bean burger with pickles and extra mustard, so he wasn't very excited by the breakfast that was laid before him. But it was real food, rather than dream food, and he dove into it, grateful that it was food at all. Then, when breakfast was over, Ideth efficiently cleaned up the dishes.

"You can wipe, Mateo," she said, offering him a small dish towel.

Mateo frowned. Was Ideth going to be just like his mother, expecting him to *help?*

"I need to pee," he muttered, heading for the mouth of the cave.

Claiming he had to go to the bathroom was a good excuse to get out of work, he'd found. No one could argue with it. And it was true, for once, so he took care of his business behind a boulder without any guilt at all.

The morning air was crisp and delightful. There was still no sound except the muffled movement of Ideth inside the cave. The beauty of the trees in the sunlight, with their low-hanging round purple fruit, made Mateo feel happy and free. He sat down on a nearby rock, picked up a stick, and began tracing letters in the dirt.

M-A-T-E-O, he wrote. T-E-N M-E-D-A-L-S! Then he scratched that out and wrote N-O S-C-H-O-O-L, which made him grin.

While Mateo spent the next half hour scratching and erasing words in the dirt, Ideth was busy packing. There wasn't much to get into her backpack—just the ducky sacks, a

few books, several pairs of reading glasses, a sewing kit, some toiletries, the hurricane lantern, some extra batteries, and her cooking gear. Her cooking pots nested inside one another (her teapot fit snuggly inside the innermost pot), so in the end her pack was very tidy and compact. She also had two special dishes for eating, which she insisted on bringing with her even though they had to be treated very carefully to prevent breaking. These she tucked inside the ducky sacks for protection. Then she cinched up the pack, slung it on her back, and was ready to go. She grabbed her flare, which she would send up as soon as they reached the beach.

When Ideth emerged from the cave, Mateo had just scratched out S-W-I-N-G! and was about to write E-M-P-O-R-O-R O-F T-H-E M-O-N-K-E-Y-S!

"Being an emperor would be so much fun, Mateo! I agree!" Ideth said, her eyes shining. "But you're about to misspell emperor. It's E-M-P-E-R-O-R, not E-M-P-O-R-O-R. Am I right or am I right?"

It was several miles down to the beach, along a complicated series of crisscrossed trails that Ideth seemed to know by heart. But it was a rather dull hike for Mateo because, other than the occasional large field of boulders and streams to cross, it was just one Finding Fruit tree after another. There were no lakes to swim in or animals to see or interesting things to pick up along the way, and because he was wearing only socks (having left his shoes back in the fine house by the sea), his feet were pretty beat up.

But Mateo kept going, hanging onto Ideth's promise of a beach at the end of their trek. And sure enough, after what seemed like an eon, he heard the distant sound of surf and crying seabirds. The forest thinned as the trail began a series of steep downhill switchbacks. At the bottom, there was a flat area where the trail widened out and the hard ground was replaced by sand. And then, like miners crawling out from a dark chasm into the light of day, he and Ideth were suddenly at the ocean, standing on the edge of an expansive beach under a wide, impossibly blue sky.

Mateo lived by the ocean back on Earth, but the beaches near his fine house were nothing as inviting as this one. It was a true tropical beach, with enormous unbroken seashells littered about as if no one had ever gone beachcombing. The tide was far out, much farther than he could ever remember seeing it at home. And there were large green tortoises with checkered shells, lumbering slowly up and down the beach, as if they were fishing (which indeed they were).

Ideth led Mateo along the beach toward a pier, which was enormously high and stretched way, way out, across the wet sand to where the surf was. They climbed up a steep ladder to reach the top and then walked several hundred feet before Ideth stopped and lit the flare. She appeared to know exactly what she was doing, because it shot far up into the azure, moons-less sky, arched motionless for a moment or two, and then lazily zig-zagged toward the distant waves until it disappeared.

"Now we'll walk out to the end of the pier and wait. It won't be long before Laup gets here. He's very dependable, the dear man," Ideth said.

Reaching the end of the pier took many more minutes because Mateo had so much to see and stopped often. There were dozens of different kinds of crabs scuttling sidewise along the beach at amazing speeds, scampering toward the pier, briefly disappearing beneath it, and then racing out the other side. There were more tortoises, some right near the pier, who eyed them curiously from below, turning their less-than-graceful heads skyward before returning to their slow trudging.

There were hundreds of shorebirds, feasting on crustaceans and other goodies brought in and dropped by the tides. And there was *sound*. Finally, sound! The air was full of it: lolling surf, squawking birds, scuttling crabs, and whispering wind.

At one point, Mateo looked behind him and gasped in awe at the beauty of the dense Finding Forest, which glittered in the sunlight along the entire shoreline, offering up its purple fruit like showy flowers.

Mateo wished he had his cell phone to take a photo and text it to his mother. She could spend hours in a place like this, taking pictures of the forest from all kinds of angles to get just the right shot. Once, she'd taken a photo of him while he was sleeping that had won an award in the local newspaper and embarrassed him almost to death. He'd been teased by his classmates and baseball buddies over that one, but now he kind of missed his mother. He wondered what she was doing and if she missed him, too.

When they reached the end of the pier, the water was nearly halfway up the pilings. It had deepened from a dazzling turquoise to a majestic blue.

"Isn't it stunning, Mateo? I'm so sorry your mother can't take a photo of it," Ideth said, dropping her backpack on the pier. "Am I right or am I right?"

"Do you have a cell phone?" Mateo asked Ideth, hopefully. "Maybe I could use yours."

"My ancestors had something like your cell phones. They called them chatterboxes. But we lost the CB towers in the great melt a long time ago, and no one has rebuilt them."

"The great melt?"

"That's right. All the ice caps at the poles melted and the sea flooded over the continents. It was a long time ago now."

"But how do you communicate with each other?" asked Mateo. "Everyone on Earth has a cell phone, even people who herd goats among the lions and giraffes in Africa. I've seen the photos."

"Well, we have paddle-saddlers who transport messages between islands and, as you've just seen, we also use flares. Some people swear by carrier gulls, but I've found them very unreliable."

"But doesn't that take a long time?"

"The paddle-saddlers are amazing athletes, Mateo. Why, they can paddle a message from Cairntip to Finding Island in only a few days. But you're right. Compared to the chatterboxes, our current methods are very slow. But I don't mind. In fact, I like it. Slowing down gives you more time to enjoy life, don't you think? I suppose some people want to speed things up again. I know a few of them on Cairntip. But most of us are content the way things are now. We can't remember the days before the great melt and it's hard to miss something you never had."

Mateo pondered this. His brother couldn't live without a cell phone or a laptop. Alex was always texting his friends and uploading stuff onto Facebook. They'd gone camping once and Alex had gone through "withdrawal" as his mother had called it. But Mateo had climbed trees and watched herons fishing in the streams, happier than he'd ever been at the fine house by the sea with all its fancy technology.

"In any case, no chatterbox photo could capture this lovely view and all the sounds and smells that go with it," observed Ideth. "So enjoy it now, before the boat comes!"

Mateo took a deep breath of the fresh sea air and lifted his face to the sun, opening up his arms as if to embrace the sky.

"Hurrah!" he cried, not really knowing why. It just felt right. Right and wonderful!

But Ideth understood. She had just given her findling with *Presence* permission to slow down and be in the here and now. And he was loving it.

Chapter 8

LAUP

Ideth had been right. They didn't have to wait long for the boat. Less than an hour after she'd shot off the flare, they were climbing onto the deck of a small sailboat, assisted by a short elderly urth man who was clearly the skipper and sole shipmate to himself.

"Greetings and welcome, welcome!" he cried cheerily as he helped Ideth off with her backpack and onto a seat behind the mainsail.

"You're on a finding, madam," he said gallantly with a sweeping bow, "and I am at your service."

Then he turned to Mateo.

"And YOU," he said, looking him up and down with unbridled enthusiasm, "*YOU* must be the findling!"

Mateo was enjoying being the apple of every eye and gave the man a wide grin.

"And she's my uppy!" he said proudly, pointing at Ideth.

"Yes indeed, she is," said the man, "and never a nobler uppy than Ideth. Why she's completed four findings, my boy! *Four!* And you'll be her fifth successful one I shouldn't wonder!"

There was something very reverent about the way the man treated Ideth, as if she was a queen and he was a nobleman who'd come to fetch her back to court in a carriage.

"Tut! Tut!" scolded Ideth. "Stop treating me like I'm royalty, Laup. We all do our jobs, uppies like me and flaremen like you. And you're the best flareman there is, Laup. You never miss a flare and you always arrive well-stocked. Everyone knows that."

"Don't listen to her boy," said Laup, turning to Mateo with a lopsided smile. "I'm just an old salt and she's an uppy!"

Then he turned back and looked searchingly at Ideth. "Which island are you headed for?"

"Krog Pad," she said decisively.

"Ah, happy be!" cried the man with a whoop and a wink at Mateo. "The gift of *Presence*, eh? You'll have a grand time on Krog Pad, and that's the truth. It's been more than a year since I visited those folks and I miss them. They always make me laugh."

In overall appearance, Laup was much like Ideth. His skin was lavender, he had webbed feet, and his hair was long and wooly. He also had the indigo layer of blubber around his middle, but unlike Ideth, he wasn't naked. He was wearing a bright yellow loincloth.

Once Laup had gotten Ideth and Mateo seated securely on the deck, he opened a hatch, disappeared below, and reappeared with a picnic basket brimming with food.

"I expect you're both more than ready for some of this," he said, placing it before them with a knowing smile.

Mateo couldn't wait to see what goodies were inside, but he was pretty sure he should let Ideth go first.

"That's it, boy!" Laup said approvingly. "It's Ideth who gets the first dip. Let her take what she likes and you can have what's left. There's plenty for you both."

Mateo nodded and then looked at Ideth, whose hands were already exploring the basket. It was quite breezy on the boat and Ideth's wiry hair was mussed up and going every which way while she tried to hold it down with her free hand.

Mateo thought the meal was delicious, especially when compared to the yucky Finding Fruit he'd been eating. He felt vaguely guilty because he was certain that the food in Laup's basket would be outlawed in the fine house by the sea. But he was so hungry that he would have eaten anything as long as it wasn't Finding Fruit. When he and Ideth were thoroughly stuffed and the goodness of the food was beginning to seep into their blood, Laup cleared away the scant leftovers and motioned toward Ideth's backpack.

"Is there anything you're missing for the training?" he asked her. "I have a variety of extra supplies on hand."

"Mateo was sunburned in outer space," she replied, "so if you have any Bitter Bugger spray, we could use some. Other than that, Krog Pad is a very basic place. We'll have no need for luxuries. And besides, you know I like travelling light. I can make do. All we need is a buoy so we can get our existing supplies to Krog Pad safely. And, of course, we need paddling gear for Mateo."

"And a cure for those Krog Padders!" Laup laughed, shaking his head as he disappeared again below deck.

Mateo could hear him rummaging around for something and, sure enough, Laup came back up a minute or two later, grunting with effort, dragging a buoy behind him, as round as a beach ball and about double the size. The buoy was attached to a rope, and at the end of the rope there was a large clip.

He tugged on the clip until the rope was taut, and grunted with satisfaction. "Here's your paddling buoy," he told Ideth. "Let's get your things inside."

Laup opened a curved door in the buoy and Ideth stuffed her backpack into the opening.

"And we'll need those clothes of yours," Laup told Mateo. "Or the wet suit won't fit properly."

Mateo looked at Ideth in alarm.

"I have to take off my clothes?" he thought loudly, opening his eyes wide and looking straight into hers.

It was the first time he'd tried to communicate directly to her with his thoughts and he found it to be quite effective.

"Just down to your underwear," Ideth whispered reassuringly. "I know you findlings don't like going naked, though I have no idea why. It feels wonderful to me. So freeing."

Mateo reluctantly removed his t-shirt, shorts, and soggy socks. His clothes were filthy now with sand and seawater and ripped in a few places. But what really embarrassed him was the pair of Mickey Mouse boxers he was wearing under his clothes. He hated them, but they were the underwear he'd been able to find the previous morning back home. They were two sizes too

small and made him look like he was a dumb baby, but there was nothing he could do about it now.

Whether out of politeness or simply because they didn't notice, Ideth and Laup didn't comment on his boxers. Instead, Laup handed him some Bitter Bugger spray, which he smeared on his skin while Laup and Ideth worked together to get his clothes into the buoy and to seal it up.

"This one won't leak!" Laup said when they were done, slapping the side of the buoy with pride.

Ideth smiled her approval. "I can always count on you, Laup. Now all we need is a harness, a mask, a snorkel, and a wetsuit and we'll be hitching up at the East End Paddling Station by dinnertime."

The harness was for Ideth and the mask, wetsuit, and snorkel were for Mateo. There were several wetsuits to choose from, and Mateo picked out a silver and black one with a shark on the side.

"I like this one," he said.

As he stared at the shark, he imagined himself riding on it, with a whip in his hand, bucking through the waves. He was a seafaring cowboy.

"Lovely, lovely!" Ideth clapped, her face brightening until it beamed. "I'm sure you'd make a grand cowboy and I love the fantasy! But, I'm afraid the shark wetsuit is a bit big for you. You need one that is nice and snug. Am I right or am I right?"

In the end, Mateo was happy with his second choice, which fit him perfectly. It was blood red and displayed a large, scary-looking octopus on the back side. Once he'd pulled it on (which took some time because the suit was so rubbery), he sat down, waiting for Laup to start the boat and whisk them away to Krog Pad, which was apparently their destination.

"Oh, we're not going to bother Laup for a ride," Ideth said, helping him to his feet again. "He's already doing us a favor by bringing us the supplies we need for paddling. The wetsuit is to keep you warm and buoyant during the swim. It's more than 60 miles to Krog Pad."

Mateo was temporarily stunned, a feeling that quickly turned to fear.

"We're going to SWIM?" he asked out loud, and when he got to the word "SWIM," he opened his eyes wide until they looked like dinner plates.

"We call it paddling, and it's perfectly safe as long as you follow my directions," Ideth replied soothingly. "With the wetsuit, mask, and snorkel, and my strong head of hair, you'll be just fine. But we'd better get started or we'll be starved by the time we arrive."

"The East End Paddling Station is mid-way to Krog Pad, so you don't have to paddle the 60 miles in one stretch," Laup explained. "But you'll still need to cover more than 25 miles, and it will take you from now until dusk. It's lucky you have such nice weather. In a storm, it might take you a week."

Inwardly, Mateo was panicking. When his parents had taught him to swim in the family pool when he was a toddler ("We want to make sure you can swim out if you fall in"), he'd barely learned the basics. Now he was faced with swimming

miles and miles in *open ocean*—and Ideth and Laup thought he could swim.

Of course they thought he could swim! All of his friends back home could swim.

"I'll bet all four of Ideth's other findlings were super swimmers," he thought in alarm. "And now Ideth and Laup assume I can swim, too. I'll have to tell them the truth or I'll drown!"

"No need to worry, dear," said Ideth, reading his mind again with a motherly smile. "Not one of my former findlings could swim before they got here. Children with *Presence* rarely learn because they're too busy daydreaming, and children who *Ignore Rules* only learn to swim if they want to, which many of them don't. I'll bet you made all kinds of excuses not to learn to swim at home. Am I right or am I right?"

Mateo nodded dismally, a feeling of suffocating dread settling over him. No matter what Ideth said, he was sure he was doomed. He was going to drown on a planet 64,000 light years from home, and there was absolutely nothing he could do about it.

Chapter 9

PADDLING WITH IDETH

Mateo had been snorkeling once in Hawaii, but only very close to shore in ridiculously safe conditions. He needed a brief reminder about how to use a snorkel (which he only half-listened to because he was so frightened) and additional instructions concerning how to *hold on*.

"You grasp it here," Ideth demonstrated, kneeling down to his level and placing his hand in a mass of hair that protruded from the back side of her scalp. There was a tuft there, he noticed, that was even coarser than the rest of her wiry black hair.

"That's the target," she instructed. "And you don't have to hold on for dear life. A firm grasp with your left hand is all that's needed. Children swim on the right."

Ideth put on the harness that Laup had given her and then deftly dove off the boat into the water. The buoy was already floating nearby, and she came up gracefully next to it. Laup was holding the clip end of the rope on deck and swung it out to her, where she caught it and attached it to her harness.

"Now it's your turn," Laup said, turning to Mateo. "I'll show you how it's done."

Laup took Mateo to the side of the boat and demonstrated how to lower himself into the ocean without getting any water into his snorkel.

Mateo's heart was thumping in his chest, but Ideth reached out for him reassuringly, and he eased himself into the water without mishap. To his surprise, the wetsuit and mask helped keep him afloat, so he barely needed to move his legs to keep his head above water. But it didn't matter if his head was above the water anyway, as long as the end of his snorkel was. In fact, with the warm water surrounding him and Ideth at his side, he didn't feel nearly as scared as he'd thought he would.

"Remember, grab my hair at the tuft with your *left* hand and swim to my right. Three tugs say 'trouble,' one tug says 'okay.' If you want to surface for a rest, tug twice. We'll be surfacing every so often so I can breathe, too. Just follow my lead. I'll do all the work."

Mateo grabbed Ideth's hair with both hands, and in the wrong place, so she gently corrected him.

"Just the left hand, Mateo. That's it. And you need to relax. It's like floating. You'll find that the tuft grabs onto you just as hard as you grab onto it, if not harder. The tufts evolved for our children to hold onto while we paddle, and they work beautifully."

Mateo grasped the tuft as directed and suddenly found himself underwater. For a moment, the world was all swirls of liquid murkiness. But then he felt a gentle tug, and he was being dragged along, just under the waves, with his snorkel clearing the surface of the water like a periscope.

As Ideth took her first few long strokes, she straightened out. And as she did so, Mateo straightened out just above and to the right of her. It all seemed very natural.

Thrust, thrust, float. Thrust, thrust, float. Thrust, thrust, float. Ideth was paddling.

Mateo's heart was banging, but he was able to breathe, and took several long deep gulps of air to make sure the system was working.

He mentally checked in. His left hand was grabbing the tuft. (Or was *it* grabbing *him?*) His mouth was sealed around the mouthpiece of the snorkel; no leaks. Ideth was just beneath him off to his left, her black hair streaming (thrust) or drifting (float).

Three tugs say 'trouble,' one tug says 'okay.' If you want to surface for a rest, tug twice. Mateo repeated the instructions to himself four times in a row, and then tugged once.

They were off.

Have you ever swum in the ocean with your eyes open and a big breath of air in your lungs? If so, I hope it was a warm ocean, like the one Mateo found himself in. In a warm ocean, the water is only a bit cooler than your own body, and it feels like a second skin rather than something separate. You feel like you're part of something huge and majestic, much bigger than yourself. But at the same time, you feel safe. It's like being wrapped in a blanket and being held by your mother.

When Mateo had snorkeled in Hawaii, it had been so baby-like—presented in a pseudo-laidback style. The instructor had shown them photographs of fish and set up a prize system to reward the "top three" children who could point them out to him in their first practice session. Mothers and fathers hovered nearby on the beach with cameras and waved encouragingly while their children entered the water. They pretended they didn't care whether their child was one of the "top three" but they all did. Many even hedged their bets.

"My little Evan is such a clown," one man said, thrusting out his chest and chuckling. "He won't be among the top three, you can bet on it."

The woman standing next to him sighed. "It's such a trial to raise a gifted child, you know. Marigold is too smart to care about competitions."

Mateo's experience with snorkeling on Urth couldn't have been more different. For one thing, it was real. It was *adult*. There was at least 50 feet of water beneath him, and if he got separated from Ideth, he was sure he'd eventually drown or get eaten. It was do or die: grab Ideth's tuft with his left hand and breathe deeply through his snorkel. He'd only known his uppy for less than 24 hours. Could he trust her? Perhaps not. He wouldn't know for sure until the paddle was over.

His parents weren't watching, either, perched on the cliff edge of disappointment, praying that he'd win a stupid game so they wouldn't be embarrassed. This wasn't about his parents at all. It was about him. This entire crazy urthshaking experience, he realized in that instant, was about *him!* It was confusing and exhilarating and scary all at once, and simply wonderful!

Mateo tugged twice and they surfaced. There was an awkward moment while Mateo spit out his snorkel.

"I just wanted to make sure two tugs worked," he apologized.

Ideth took several very long, deep breaths.

"Good for you!" she finally replied with an approving nod. "It's always a good idea to make sure you're safe and understand the rules."

They bobbed on the surface for a minute or two, but there was nothing much to see. The ocean stretched off in all directions, with no sight of land.

"I'm going to have to start navigating," Ideth told him. "And it will feel rather strange to you. I send out sound waves so I can see the ocean floor around us."

"Like radar?" asked Mateo.

"Exactly!" replied Ideth approvingly. "The thing is, you won't be able to hear the sounds I make. They're out of range of your hearing. But you'll be able to feel them. You'll see what I mean once we get going again. Just don't be alarmed."

Mateo put his snorkel back in his mouth and straightened it. Then he tugged once on Ideth's tuft. Ideth took in another big breath, let about half of it out, and then dropped beneath the waves.

It was only a few moments later that Mateo felt the tingling along his skin that told him that Ideth was navigating. As they swam along, the tingling would come and go, and Mateo could sense Ideth changing directions as she "saw" the landscape of the ocean floor beneath them and led them expertly in the direction of the East End Paddling Station.

There's no way I can do justice to the colors, sizes, and numbers of fishes that Mateo saw as they paddled their way east that day. Sometimes a school would appear and surround them and the next moment it would be gone. Most of the action was on the reef below, and Mateo eventually became relaxed enough to enjoy the show.

They surfaced several more times for Ideth to breathe. There was only one time that he briefly felt like tugging on her tuft three times, but the shark passed before he had time to do it.

It was noon by the time Mateo realized that he was ravenous, and it worried him. When they'd set out, he hadn't considered how they would eat on the road (so to speak). With a full belly, it's hard to imagine having an empty one. By the time you do, it's hard to imagine that it was ever full.

What follows is an abbreviated account of the sloppy, watery lunch that ensued as they bobbed about in the open ocean: *Yuk*. It wasn't much, and Mateo was almost as hungry afterwards as he'd been when they'd begun. But it was something rather than nothing, and it would have to do. They drank water too, before returning everything back to the buoy for the final leg of their trip.

Thrust, thrust, float. Thrust, thrust, float. Thrust, thrust, float.

It seemed to go on forever. Mateo had some wonderful fantasies along the way, however—richly embellished ones where he played the role of a plundering pirate of the East Seas, a coral cowboy, and a castaway who was really a prince. The sun

sank into the western sky behind them and the water turned a deep blue-gold. Mateo was starting to think that Ideth was lost, when she suddenly surfaced and did her deep breathing routine one last time.

"About 10 minutes now," she said when she was done. "We're almost there."

They returned to paddling and, just as promised, the East End Paddling Station came into view a few minutes later.

"It's more like a submarine than a station," thought Mateo as Ideth changed directions to avoid hitting one of the mighty cables that held the Station in place.

The underground portion of the building was four stories high and brightly painted. One wall was covered in colorful ocean scenes, while another sported a youthful urth woman offering up a conch full of food. As they swam closer, the details of the building became clearer, and Mateo could see a line of portholes on each floor.

Ideth paddled them over to a ladder, which extended several feet into the water from a broad platform above. When they reached it, she helped Mateo get his footing and then gave his bottom a boost so he could grab the rails. The platform rocked and it took Mateo two tries to get out of the water and onto the deck. But once he was safe, he was able to sit down, remove his mask and snorkel, shake the water out of his hair, and look around.

Ideth was close behind him.

"Well done, findling," she said, as she plopped down beside him. "You've completed your first paddle! Wasn't that fun?"

Mateo grinned and was about to tell Ideth about the shark he'd seen, but he was interrupted before he could even begin.

"Welcome to the East Ender!" remarked an urth woman who'd seen them arrive. She walked up to them with a clipboard. "Do you have a reservation, or is this a paddle-by?"

"It's a paddle-by," replied Ideth with a warm smile. "Could you please stow our buoy and assign us a cabin? We've just paddled 25 miles from Finding Island, and we're completely starved."

Chapter 10

A BERTH AT
THE EAST ENDER

T he East End Paddling Station, it turned out, was an underwater hotel! Mateo was so excited to get to their cabin that he could hardly contain himself. The "above board" floor of the station was a reception area enclosed by a glass dome that looked as if it had seen better days. But it was a hotel in the middle of the ocean, after all, and got pooped on by sea birds and weathered by wind and rain. Someone had affixed a stuffed owl to the top of the dome in a futile attempt to keep the birds away, but there was a gull preening its feathers right on top of the owl's fuzzy head.

"It's a Cairntip gull-eating owl," Ideth told Mateo with a snort. "And you can see all the bloody good it's doing."

"One room, twin berths, ocean view. One uppy and one findling. We'll put you in the Seahorse Room."

The woman with the clipboard directed a teenage boy to secure their buoy. Then the boy unloaded the contents of their buoy into a large plastic "guest tub," and disappeared down a hole at the back of the reception building.

"Dinner's included for findlings," the woman with the clipboard continued, with a nod at Mateo.

"And your stay, madam," she added, with a slight bow to Ideth, "is entirely free, of course. We won't be charging the Uppy Council a single Cairntip tidbit for the honor of having you as a guest."

The "hole" led down a narrow winding staircase that connected the above-board floor with the cabins below. Before he followed Ideth down, Mateo glanced into the station dining room, where there was a long table covered with white linen. A whiteboard announced "Dinner served promptly at seven. Loincloths respectfully suggested."

Their room was even more amazing than Mateo had hoped. The walls were covered with murals of seahorses and the shelves were lined with books about them: *All the Urth's Seahorses, Seahorses of the Southern Islands, My Mommy's a Seahorse!* (The last was a book for toddlers, Mateo noticed, and rather silly.)

Along one side of the room was a set of bunkbeds, and each had a little porthole at the pillow end so the occupant could see out into the surrounding ocean.

"We're at sea, so our beds are called berths," Ideth told him. "Would you like the top berth or the bottom?"

Mateo wanted the top berth, and Ideth let him have it. But there was the problem of his wet suit, which clearly had to come off, and his lack of clean clothes to replace it.

"Your clothes are in among these things but they're filthy," Ideth said, rummaging through the guest tub. "We can give them to the staff to launder, but we're going to need loincloths for dinner. I'll see if I can find a pair of sandals for you, too. It's dangerous to go barefoot at a paddling station. There may be loose nails."

Ideth disappeared briefly, returning only a few minutes later with two loincloths, a green one for Mateo and a blue one for her, and a pair of human beach sandals that looked as if they were about to fall apart.

"I think more than a few findlings have borrowed these over the years," Ideth laughed. "But they'll do in a pinch."

There was a small bathroom in their quarters with just enough room for Mateo to remove his wetsuit and boxers, take a quick shower ("Scrub!" shouted Ideth from behind the closed door), and put on the loincloth. But donning the loincloth was difficult for Mateo. He had never worn one before and had no idea how to loop it around and secure it. He'd seen Laup in one, but the more ways he tried folding it around his midsection and up through his legs, the more confused he became.

"Need help!'" he called out. "But don't look!"

"Oh, don't be silly," Ideth replied dismissively. "I know all about your anatomy. But I know you like your privacy, so I'll just demonstrate on myself. It's easy once you watch someone else do it."

Mateo stuck his head out from around the bathroom door to watch. Ideth picked up her own loincloth, shook it out, and then showed Mateo, step-by-step, how to put it on. Ideth didn't appear to have any private parts as far as Mateo could tell and he wondered why not.

"They're up inside where you can't see them," she explained, reading his mind. "That's why we don't care about going naked. No one can see anything anyway."

Mateo disappeared into the bathroom again and reemerged about two minutes later, the loincloth well-tied and hanging just as it should.

Ideth stood back and admired him as the station swayed ever so slightly beneath their feet.

"You're starting to look like a proper urthling!" she said approvingly. "I'll take my shower now and you can explore your berth. I'll be out in a jiffy."

Mateo climbed up to the top berth and peered through the porthole to look into the sea. It was that same eerie twilight he'd experienced the night before, right before moons-rise, but there were external floodlights on the hotel that suddenly sputtered to life and gave him a view of some of the creatures lurking in the murky waters. A grouper-like fish swam up to the window and stared at him, hanging in the swaying water as if to appraise this new station guest. Mateo tapped on the glass, which did not seem to impress the fish. It darted away almost instantly and disappeared into the blue beyond.

The berth was extremely comfortable.

"Best ducky sacks on Urth," said Ideth, when she got out of the shower and was cinching up her loincloth. "Like sinking into butter."

Ideth lay down on her berth for a "quick bit of shut-eye" while Mateo lay on his back and put his legs straight up in the air. He could flatten his heels against the ceiling when his legs were in this position, and getting them upside down felt very refreshing after the long day's paddle. He hadn't done much of the hard work, of course, but he was tired nonetheless.

"I'm the captain of this station," he day-dreamed. "A pirate captain who steals from the rich and gives to the poor!"

Mateo envisioned himself with a black patch over one eye.

"Above deck duty!" he shouted to a seaman. "Time to get us some loot!"

Mateo smiled as he pictured himself with a peg leg. He'd be Long Mateo Silver, he decided, supreme captain of his own ship: the Ship of Presents.

His mind paused.

"Why the Ship of *Presents?*" he asked himself. It had something to do with what Laup had said on the boat. *The gift of presents.* And Ideth had said something about findlings having gifts the first time they had met one another, in the cave.

Mateo's tummy was grumbling, and he was counting the minutes until dinner, but in the meantime he pondered his situation.

He was a findling. Ideth was his uppy. He had a *gift— the gift of presents*, which seemed like a redundant gift. Presents were already gifts. And he was headed to an island with the weirdest name ever that had funny people on it that Laup liked.

But why were they going there? And why was he on Urth anyhow? How could a crack in a bedroom ceiling lead to another planet on the other side of the galaxy with two moons and a paddling station that was an underwater hotel?

Mateo pondered his plight for another few moments, but he didn't focus on the conundrum for very long. He was soon distracted by a splendid fantasy of being a tattooed sailor bearing heaps of Christmas presents for poor urthling children. Then a gong sounded from somewhere above them, and Ideth interrupted his reverie.

"That's the dinner bell," she cried enthusiastically, sitting up suddenly and banging her head on the underside of Mateo's berth.

"Bother!" she cried out, rubbing her head. "I always seem to do that when I sleep here. Why do my findlings always want the top berth?"

Mateo climbed down, looking at Ideth rather guiltily. Perhaps he shouldn't have asked for the top berth. Ideth had done all the hard work paddling, after all, and now she'd bumped her head.

"And, by the way," Ideth added, rather testily, "it's P-R-E-S-E-N-C-E, not P-R-E-S-E-N-T-S. If you're a tattooed sailor on a mission of mercy, you need to know the difference. Am I right, or am I right?"

Chapter 11

SHUM

The hotel was lightly populated. There were only two other guests to be exact. One was a trader named Watler from Cairntip, who was selling Finding Fruit ("the best this side of Finding Island") in exchange for almost anything else.

"No takers here," Ideth told him, as she winked at Mateo.

The other guest was a young, goofy-looking man named Shum who grinned at them with his tongue hanging out, and had to be calmed down several times (though not unkindly) by the waitress.

"Let's leave it for now, Shum," she chastised him repeatedly.

"Happy be! Food for me!!" Shum shouted, bouncing up and down in his chair.

Mateo was immediately entranced and found himself bouncing too.

"Shum's on his way home to Krog Pad tomorrow, thank goodness," whispered the waitress to Ideth. "I've had just about as much of that duppy as I can stand."

The waitress was the same friendly woman who had checked them in when they'd arrived, but she looked haggard now.

"Don't I know it," Ideth whispered back. "We'll be on Krog Pad for the next few Lunera months at least, and I'm having to steel myself."

"I thought so," said the waitress, turning her gaze briefly in Mateo's direction. "The gift of *Presence*. You can see it in those soulful eyes of his."

There were no menus. The food was served family style, with dishes appearing spontaneously at regular intervals and in no apparent order.

"It doesn't matter where you start," Ideth told Mateo, as she helped herself to some soup. "You arrive in the same place: satisfied!"

Shum was so beside himself at the sight of food that he leapt up and almost upset the steaming bowl of lightly broiled shrimp in the waitress' hands. Sternly, she asked him to leave the table.

"PLEASE, Shum! Give the others a chance to get started!"

Amazingly, Shum slunk away to stand at the side of the room, looking remorseful, but with his eyes still fixed on the food. Once Ideth, Watler, and Mateo had served themselves, Shum was allowed to return.

"Manners!" the waitress hissed, and Shum calmed down as she heaped some food onto his plate.

"Been paddling for three weeks," Watler grumbled as he dug in. "The business was good at first but now it's fallen off. My buoy's still full of Finding Fruit and it's starting to go bad.

Shouldn't be telling you that, of course, but I can see you're fresh back from Finding Island and you'll not be interested."

"Me fruit have!" Shum shouted, jumping up once more. His chair fell backwards onto the floor and he smiled ecstatically. "Happy be!"

"*NO*, Shum!" cried the waitress, as she flew back into the room from the galley. "You don't want to sleep outside on the deck again, do you? You'll be forced to, you know, if you keep acting this way!"

Shum looked at her and immediately slumped back into his seat, a look of deep shame on his face, while the waitress turned to the other guests apologetically.

"Mr. Shum has an excitable temperament," she explained, "but a heart of gold."

Shum looked up tentatively and then broke into another wide grin.

"But you need to control yourself," she added, turning to look at him again, with a frown. "Now I think we understand one another."

She threw Ideth an exasperated look as she cleared some of the bowls and prepared to bring in more.

"It's because they never get food like this on Krog Pad," observed Watler. "No cooking."

Shum lowered his eyes.

"It's all right, fella," Watler went on, in a gentler tone. "Not your fault. Born into that culture. Never learned the value of a solid day's work."

"But their culture has a fine purpose!" Ideth pointed out, defensively. "A noble one!"

Shum looked up, hopefully.

"Yes, I suppose that's right," said Watler. "I forgot about that." And his eyes swept past Ideth and Shum to Mateo.

"It do! It do!" cried Shum, alight again. "Happy be run! Beach be free!"

"Yes, well," said Watler. "I'm just glad you have your own beaches and aren't running around on Cairntip's. No offense."

Shum slumped.

"Well, you can have your Cairntip beaches, Watler, because we're going to Krog Pad after we leave here, aren't we, Mateo?" responded Ideth, giving Shum a warm smile.

"You bet we are!" agreed Mateo delightedly. "I want to run on the beach with you, Shum!"

Shum could barely contain himself, shaking with the effort to keep himself from leaping up again. "We! We!" he said in short breaths, as he looked toward the waitress, who was glowering at him.

After dinner, everyone stepped out onto the deck and watched the moons-rise. The moons rose a little later than the night before, and Lunera lagged behind Ru.

"They're pulling apart," Ideth explained. "In a couple of days, we won't be seeing Lunera in the evening sky any longer."

Shum began running up and down, excitedly pointing at the moons. He even leapt into the water at one point, rising happily to the surface with an enormous smile, as if Urth's

moons were new to him and the most wonderful things you could imagine.

When they got back to their room, Ideth handed Mateo a little pad and a pencil.

"It's for sketching," she told him.

Mateo cocked his head to one side. He didn't think he was very artistic—at least not on paper. All his images were stored up in his head. But he decided to give it a try. It took him half an hour, but by the end he'd made a decent sketch of Ideth.

"Looks just like me," Ideth assured him, though she thought it made her look too skinny and a great deal too human.

They crawled into their berths to go to sleep.

Mateo burrowed into his ducky sack and sighed happily.

"This has been the best day of my life," he thought. "I don't want it to end!"

In truth, however, he was completely exhausted, like a toddler after too much time at Disneyland. And the gentle rock, rock, slush of the East End Paddling Station felt soothing, like a mother's heartbeat.

Mateo's eyes closed and soon he was asleep. His body lay in a berth at the East Ender, 64,000 light years from home, under the watchful gaze of two alien moons. But, in his dreams, he was laughing in the sunlight, running down a beach on Krog Pad Island, with Shum leaping enthusiastically beside him.

Chapter 12

MATEO'S RENAMING

The next morning, at breakfast, Shum was notably absent.

"He left early this morning," explained the waitress. "I filled up his buoy with food last night, hoping he'd take the hint."

Mateo was disappointed. The table conversation was much less interesting without Shum in the mix. Ideth and Watler droned on about import taxes, politics, and the "ridiculously inflated" cost of inland caves on Cairntip.

Mateo ate two helpings of everything and then wandered back to the Seahorse Room. He wanted to text his friends and brag about his adventures, but his cell phone was back in Monterey, out of battery life, and in the hands of the police (though he didn't know that).

I'm sorry to tell you that he did not think of texting his poor parents. Instead, he experimented with how long he could hold a headstand.

When Ideth found him, his record was more than 15 seconds—not bad on a gently rocking floor. The only problem was that his loincloth flipped forward into his face when he was upside down. Even though his private parts were still covered (urthling loincloths manage that in all positions), he felt oddly exposed. When he heard Ideth coming down the hallway, he immediately shot up the ladder to his berth and pretended to be examining a mole on his arm.

"Fifteen seconds is astounding!" said Ideth as she entered the room. "Am I right or am I right?"

She headed into the bathroom and emerged, naked. "So much for loincloths," she said. "They're a nightmare."

Mateo looked at her with a pout on his face.

"I miss Shum," he said glumly.

"No worries," Ideth replied. "If things go as planned, we'll be seeing him before the day is out. No doubt he paddled straight to Krog Pad and is waiting for us already. There are no paddling stations between here and there, and even if there were, it's unlikely he'd be welcome. Most stations turn away Krog Padders, you know. Closed-minded, if you ask me."

Mateo couldn't imagine anyone disliking Shum. Watler, maybe. He was a bit of a bore. But not Shum.

"In any event," added Ideth briskly, "before we pack up and leave, you need to choose a new name. We can't leave for Krog Pad until you've renamed yourself. Those are the rules."

"Rename myself?" asked Mateo, sitting up. Ideth hadn't told him about this yet.

"Yes, indeed! And the quicker the sooner! I brought along a set of Renaming Letters and it's time you got busy."

Ideth explained the process to Mateo, and he was especially excited when she told him that children have more control over their lives afterwards.

"Happy be!" he shouted, leaping off his berth, running around the room, mimicking Shum.

"There'll be plenty of time for that," laughed Ideth. "Now come get your letters."

Mateo settled back into his berth, lying on his tummy. The Renaming Letters were small squares of wood, about one inch on each side, which looked a lot like Scrabble pieces. He picked up the five letters in M-A-T-E-O and began to shuffle them around with his fingers, considering each possibility in turn.

M-A-T-O-E. "Mah-toe."

"Hmmm. Sounds too much like 'my toe,'" he thought, gazing out his porthole.

A barracuda-like fish appeared in the glass and then drained away.

"No, I don't like it," he decided. "I'm the only one around here who has earthling toes and it would draw attention to them."

He tried again.

A-T-O-M-E. "Atom-E." Not bad. Images of a super-hero saving the world from an atom bomb popped into his head. He imagined himself in an hero's red cape, leaping from paddling station to paddling station, rescuing desperate urth-lings from aliens who planned to annihilate them with enormous lasers.

"Tut, tut. No war images," Ideth called out from across the room, where she was whisking about organizing their things.

"Oh, bother!" she muttered. "I forgot your laundry. Be right back."

Mateo began again. A-T-E-M-O. He bit his lip. Would it be pronounced "A-tem-o" or "Ate-mo"? Some people would pronounce it "Ate-mo," he was sure, and make fun of him for having such a big appetite. His parents were always talking about it. *He scarfed up all the leftovers, again,* was a familiar refrain in the fine house by the sea. Or: *Was that a third helping, Mateo? You must have a hollow leg to put it in!* No, he'd have to choose something else.

He tried again. O-M-A-T-E. "O-Mate." Acceptable, but maybe there was something better.

T-A-M-E-O. "Tameo." Sounds too much like a girl's name.

E-O-M-A-T. What? Too hard to pronounce.

A-M-T-O-E. "Am Toe." Definitely *not.* Even worse than "Mah-toe!"

And then it struck him.

"M-E-A-T-O!" he snickered aloud. "Meato." His parents would *hate* that name. They never let him eat meat. And, with that irony, he giggled and giggled until his tummy hurt.

By the time Ideth returned to the Seahorse Room, Meato had printed out his new name in large letters on his sketch pad, which he held up for her to see.

"I *love* it!" she clapped, dropping Meato's clean clothes into the guest tub. "It's *PERFECT!* I think your mother and father wouldn't like that name much, would they? So you chose well, my findling!"

"Have we been eating meat?" he asked.

"Not in the way you mean. When we lost all our continents, including all our farm land, we had to give it up. Now, everything we eat is from the sea in one form or another. We still raise animals for their wool and so forth, but that's all."

Meato frowned. Seafood? Is that what they'd been eating? Maybe they'd been eating seaweed, too. Gross!

"Don't worry about it," Ideth said with a knowing smile, patting him on the knee. "I'm a good cook and I know all about feeding a hungry boy like you."

Meato considered this. He had to admit that the food they'd eaten thus far, other than the Finding Fruit of course, had been yummy.

"Just don't tell me what's in it, okay?"

"Don't be silly. You'll get used to it after awhile. It's what happens when you have no other options."

Meato suddenly remembered a movie he'd seen about a man who was lost at sea in a little boat and had nothing to eat but raw fish. At first, the man had been disgusted and could barely keep it down. But as the days passed he'd found it increasingly delicious. In fact, by the time he was rescued he'd developed a great fondness for barracuda eyes.

"I won't eat fish eyes," Meato said, wanting to make that point perfectly clear, "or brains."

"No worries," Ideth assured him, "I won't try to feed you any, though some people think they're a delicacy. Shum likes them sure enough. I saw him gobbling them up last night at dinner."

"Shum!" Meato cried, suddenly remembering where they were headed and forgetting all about food. "Can we go to Krog Pad now?"

"That's the plan," Ideth affirmed. "But I tossed those silly Mickey Mouse boxers of yours. I knew you wouldn't mind. You can wear your loincloth under your wetsuit instead."

Meato danced around the cabin in excitement.

"I love paddling!" he cried. "Today is going to be fun!"

Ideth smiled in amusement, recalling how terrified Meato had been of paddling just the day before.

"Then let's be off!" she said, "and make good time. There's some weather brewing that may come our way."

They worked together to get everything into the guest tub. Then Ideth got the attention of one of the East Ender employees, who carried the tub up to the deck.

"Stock our buoy and make sure it's sealed up tight," Ideth instructed him, as they followed. "We don't want a leak, especially with possible foul weather."

When they got to the deck, the weather looked fine, as far as Meato could tell. But Ideth seemed nervous. She licked her finger and held it up, trying to gauge the direction of the wind, muttering something about "the coming monsoon season."

"Is everything okay?" Meato asked. If Ideth was anxious about the weather, he should be terrified!

"Tell me the paddling rules," she said, ignoring his question.

"One tug says 'okay,' two says 'surface,' three says 'trouble.'"

"Good boy," she replied, helping him into his wetsuit. "I think the weather will hold. Let's try and enjoy our paddle to Krog Pad. If all goes well, we'll get there by mid-afternoon and we can set up camp before moons-rise. It's time for you to meet your duppies."

"Duppies?" asked Meato. He remembered hearing the word once before.

"You'll see," Ideth said mysteriously, as she hitched up her harness, clipped it to the sealed buoy, and entered the water. "Shum is a duppy and Krog Pad is full of them. You're going to get to know each and every one."

Chapter 13

ON KROG PAD ISLAND

Meato stood on the shores of Krog Pad Island, amazed at the welcome he and Ideth were receiving. They hadn't crawled out onto the beach for more than 30 seconds before dozens of wildly enthusiastic Krog Padders were racing toward them from all directions.

"HAPPY BE! HAPPY BE!" they cried in joyous chorus as they surrounded the dripping visitors. "Look at she!" "Look at he!" "You and we! Happy be!" They leapt, dove into the water, raced up and down the beach, and made such a noise that Meato found it almost impossible to hear what Ideth was saying to him.

"DON'T ENCOURAGE YOUR DUPPIES, MEATO!" Ideth shouted over the din. "IF YOU STAY CALM, THEY'LL QUIET DOWN!"

Meato tried to remain unruffled in the midst of the chaos, but when he saw Shum charging toward him from far up the beach, he threw open his arms and ran as fast as he could towards him. They fell into a heap on the beach and Shum gave him a big wet kiss on his forehead.

"MATEO see!" Shum all but choked, weeping with joy.

"I'm Meato now!" Meato replied, thumping at his chest proudly. I renamed myself!"

Then he joined in the dancing and leaping with the rest of them: men, women, and children all mixed up together in a whirlwind of fevered exuberance, leaving Ideth to fend for herself.

Ideth sighed. "It's going to be a long training, no matter how many Lunera months it lasts," she grumbled to herself as she headed alone toward the cliffs across the hot sand, dragging the buoy behind her. It was very heavy when it was out of the water.

"Of course, no one will offer to help me get this buoy to safety," she thought testily. "If I leave the buoy close to shore, it will get carried away by the outgoing tide."

She struggled for a good half hour, huffing and puffing with the effort, before she reached the bottom of the limestone cliffs that rose in the center of Krog Pad Island. Then she unhitched the buoy and sat down for a rest.

She thought back on their paddle that day. Unlike the one the day before, it had been difficult. There had been strong winds, making the ocean rough, and Meato had struggled to keep his snorkel clear.

"If only these humans could store oxygen in their muscles like we can," she thought. "It would make things so much easier on us uppies."

Ideth looked down the beach, where Meato was leaping about with the Krog Padders. Then she looked behind her, at the towering bluff. It was up to her, she knew, to find a suit-

able cave to stow their supplies before it got dark. The Krog Padders would take them all otherwise. They had no manners. None. Especially around food.

Ideth was an expert on caves. She'd lived in them all her life and knew exactly what she was looking for. The cave needed to be high up, well above the place where the water might come even if there was a storm and a syzygy at the same time, when the tides were as high as they ever got.

The Krog Pad duppies were too preoccupied with having fun to do the hard work of finding and maintaining safe, permanent villages. They hadn't built any trails up the cliffs to connect the caves with the beach.

"Be no storm, need no trails!" they liked to say, grinning up at the wide blue sky as if it would always remain that way.

But when the storms came, they had no place to go. They had no caves when they needed them because they never built them before they were needed.

"Such stupidity!" Ideth thought in disgust. "But there's no changing them. Goodness knows people have tried. The missionaries were the worst! They forced the Krog Padders to wear full-body loincloths in this warm weather. But the Krog Padders just tore them off as soon as the missionaries turned their backs, crying *No see now!*—running off in the opposite direction, naked and jubilant."

There was a trick to spotting good places to forge trails. Ideth scanned the cliffs, considering her options. Like all Cairntip children, she'd been taught to climb almost as soon as she could walk.

"It's silly that the Krog Padders don't learn to climb," she thought. "It's because their parents don't teach them when their brains are ready, and the window of opportunity is lost."

Just before sunset, Ideth had found a good cave. It was high up, and the trail to it, while treacherous, was something she was sure Meato could handle if he was careful. The cave had a nice fissure for venting the smoke from her fire, and the floor sloped away, so that any rain that came through the fissure would run downhill and out. She spent the last hour of daylight transporting most of the supplies from the buoy up the steep bluff and into their new home.

"You don't have time to organize things now," she told herself, looking around at the inside of the cave with displeasure. "Yes, it's messy but just stop thinking about it! You can put everything away and tidy up later. There's no hurry."

Ideth picked her way back down to the beach, where she'd left the empty buoy and some basic supplies. They'd sleep on the beach the first few nights, and she'd guard everything like a hawk.

She made a campsite up against the cliffs. They'd have no shelter but she had the ducky sacks, a cooking pot, and shellfish from the tide pools. There would be no feasting, but it would get them through.

Her tummy rumbled. The only part of her job that she didn't like was going without proper meals. From the finding through the training, it was hard to plan elaborate menus like she did back home. But that was how it was, and it was worth it. When she got back to Cairntip, she'd make up for lost time,

just like she always did. The restaurants there were the finest on urth, especially the "all you can eat" places, which is where she hung out most of the time.

Ideth walked along the base of the cliff in search of Meato, keeping her eye on their campsite the whole time. She found him sitting, confused, in the middle of a circle of snoring Krog Padders. He was shaking Shum, who was practically comatose, his tongue hanging out of his mouth, his legs splayed.

"They ate a bunch of shellfish and then they just flopped," said Meato. "They haven't moved since."

"It's no use trying to wake up your duppies," Ideth told him. "They'll be sleeping like that for hours. That's what they do when evening comes on. They'll snooze all night, moonslight or no. At least they know enough to sleep up near the cliffs where they're likely to be safe from the tides. I guess they'd all be dead by now if they hadn't learned that much."

She sighed. "Let's go snug up for the night, findling. You can play with the Krog Padders again tomorrow."

The sun had dipped below the horizon now and there wouldn't be any moons-light for another hour. Ru would rise first, and Lunera would follow an hour or two later.

"Lunera is rocky, like your moon," Ideth told Meato as they picked their way along the shoreline, heading back to the buoy. "But Ru is mostly iron and metal, like a meteorite, and though it looks smaller in the sky, it's actually more massive. Lunera is the closer of the two, but I suspect you already guessed that. Lunera circles Urth in half the time that Ru does, so it goes through its phases faster. You'll see."

"What are we going to do here on Krog Pad?" Meato asked curiously. "Can I play with my duppies all day?"

"That's the idea," replied Ideth.

"I've read stories about kids who have adventures," Meato probed hopefully, "and they always learn a martial art or how to us a saber. Or kickboxing. That would be awesome! Could you teach me how to kickbox?"

Ideth laughed. "I wouldn't know what to do with a saber if I saw one and I certainly don't know how to kickbox! Can you imagine *me* kickboxing? Much too violent. I prefer cliff-diving when I have the time."

Meato didn't much like the idea of cliff-diving, whatever that was. It meant *water*, he was sure, and his recent swim with Ideth from the East Ender to Krog Pad had been uncomfortable and scary, not at all like the first day, when he'd had fun. He'd gotten seasick and had vomited twice.

"In any event," Ideth continued as she sat down on her ducky sack, crossed her skinny legs, and leaned over to light the campfire she'd prepared, "I really have no idea what will happen while you're here on Krog Pad. I really don't. We uppies never know what's going to happen. It depends on you and your duppies. You don't even need to camp with me if you don't want to. It's up to you."

Meato remained standing. "You mean I can camp with the Krog Padders all night? I don't have to stay here?"

"No, you don't," replied Ideth. "You've renamed yourself so you're free to leave anytime you want. I'm not holding

you prisoner. I might have stopped you if you were still Mateo, but you're Meato now."

"Yay!" shouted Meato, grabbing his ducky sack. It was the dark end of twilight, but he was sure he could find his way back to Shum and his friends if he left right that minute.

"But you might want to stay for supper," Ideth offered, stirring the fire, splitting open some oysters, and putting them in a pot. "The Krog Padders eat everything raw. They have no idea how to cook. They live like savages."

Meato looked at her and blinked. She was right, he decided. The idea of raw seafood made him feel a little woozy, especially after his tummy upset on the paddle.

"Well, I'll eat my meals here," Meato agreed, spreading out his ducky sack again and looking at the oysters with interest. "But I'll spend the rest of my time with my duppies, having fun!"

"I thought you might prefer to eat with me," replied Ideth with a knowing smile. "Would you like your oysters with butter or oil? I prefer the oil myself, fresh pressed from the Spaghetti Willow trees on Wannabe Island. Watler had some to sell, you know, and I couldn't resist. I think you'll like it."

Meato thought for a moment. Back home in Monterey, his parents usually used olive oil or worse yet, flax seed oil. Butter was a luxury reserved for spaghetti and pancakes, if he was lucky.

"Butter it is then," said Ideth, reading his mind again. "But just to warn you, it's not butter made from milk. We don't use domestic mammals for anything but their wool, remember?

Pot-nut butter is made from the pellets of Amdar Pot-Nut owls. After the rodent bones have been removed, that is."

Meato was disgusted and quickly changed his mind. "Ugh!" he cried.

"Well you can't expect things on Urth to be exactly like you're used to back home," Ideth responded defensively. "I'll bet you'll get hooked on the Spaghetti Willow oil anyway. Some people say it's addictive, you know, and I half believe it."

"It's made from a plant, right?" Meato asked cautiously. He'd been duped into thinking that Pot-nut butter came from a nut. He didn't want to make that kind of mistake again.

Ideth smiled. "Yes, and a beautiful one. Spaghetti Willows grow on the topside of Wannabe Island. They're like your redwoods; very rare. So the oil harvesters have to be careful and tap only a few of the trees at a time. That's why the oil is so expensive."

"I want to try it," said Meato. "It sounds good."

"Just don't let the Krog Padders have any," Ideth replied, "or we'll have a heap of trouble. They'll kick up a real fuss if they know we have it and aren't willing to share. There's nothing more annoying than a hungry Krog Padder."

"Or a hungry uppy!" Meato thought, grinning to himself.

"You're right," replied Ideth with a laugh, giving Meato a friendly shove. "Or a hungry findling!"

CHAPTER 14

MEATO ON THE BLUFFS

Ideth saw very little of Meato the first week. The weather was delightful. He played with Shum and his other exuberant duppies all day and scooted back to Ideth's camp for meals before taking off again. On the third night, he'd started sleeping with his duppies, carrying his ducky sack to their flop site high on the beach under the shadow of the towering bluffs. With Lunera rising after midnight, and Ru in its waning gibbous phase ("lit on the left," Ideth pointed out to him), he was able to get to sleep when it was still dark and stay asleep, most nights, until sunrise.

Once, he woke in the early morning, after both moons had risen, having to pee. "How weird," he thought as he took care of his business behind a rock. "Moons-light seems normal to me now."

On the eighth day, Ideth changed course. She'd been able to get the cave all comfy and ship-shape, stocked with plenty of firewood, fresh water, and enough shellfish and crabs to make Cairntip seafood chowder, one of her favorite dishes. She was tired of sleeping on the beach and eating anemic meals, and it was time to move.

So when she fed Meato his breakfast, she laid out her plans for the day.

"I've prepared us a cushy cave," she told him, pointing to a high point on the bluff. "We'll have seafood chowder and hot Win-Nin up there tonight. What do you say? Win-Nin beans grow all over the topside of this island. When they're dried properly, they taste just like chocolate, only better."

At first, Meato was enthusiastic.

"I'm ready for new food too!" he cried, clapping his hands. "And I'm a really good climber."

In truth, Meato had gone to the Spidering-Up Climbing Gym in Monterey exactly once, and had barely made it up the beginner's wall.

"Climbing the bluffs will be different than climbing in a gym," Ideth warned him, reading Meato's mind yet again. "You really have to watch your step and there will be no ropes to catch you if you fall."

"I can do it," replied Meato confidently. "I'm not a baby."

Halfway up the bluff, however, he refused to go any further.

"Why do we need to come all the way up here?" he whined, huffing and puffing. "It's too hard!"

Ideth said encouraging things to Meato, but he turned a deaf ear.

"I'm going down," he said defiantly, his knees shaking. He was scared by the steepness of the terrain, which was getting more precipitous by the minute.

Ideth shrugged. "The chowder and hot Win-Nin will be waiting for you in the cave. You can choose to join me or not. I'll leave little rock cairns along the way and if you follow those, you're sure to end up in the right spot. The choice is yours: yummy chowder and hot Win-Nin with me or raw shellfish on the beach with Shum and his friends."

"You're mean!" snapped Meato angrily.

"I'm practical," replied Ideth. "If we don't move to the cave, we'll not be safe. I can't make your decision for you, but I've made mine."

"But climbing this cliff is too scary! I'm not having any fun like I do with Shum!"

"I wouldn't give you a task I didn't think you could do, Meato. I believe you can do this if you decide to, even if it's difficult. Just keep on climbing and rest when you need to. Lean into the fear. Be brave."

Ideth handed him a water flask, turned, and continued her way up.

Meato watched her go with a look of self-righteous rage mixed with fear.

"My real parents wouldn't abandon me like this!" he shouted, his face flushing red. "I hate you!" But his voice was lost to the wind.

Meato sat down on a boulder and looked down at the beach far below. From his high vantage point, he felt strangely dizzy and he clung to a nearby boulder to steady himself. Even so, he could see that the Krog Padders were beginning to stir.

"I don't need old Ideth and her cave," he told himself. "I'm going to go back down and play sand wars with Shum."

But when he tried to pick his way back down the cliff to join them, he found it very hard to keep his footing. He almost took a nasty fall, so he had to slow down and think his way through the problem.

"If I go a bit further that way," he thought, looking off to the right, "it looks like I can squeeze between two boulders and get down to a flat area."

He headed for the boulders, but found the slender notch between them to be impassable. He couldn't descend the bluff that way, he decided. But there was another possible opening down a gully to his left, and he headed for it.

Up close, though, the gully emptied into a dizzying expanse of open air that made his heart race and his head dizzy.

"I'd better go back to where Ideth left me," he thought. "I'll have to retrace our path back to the beach from there."

But when he turned around, he couldn't figure out where the two large boulders were. He'd lost his landmarks. There were dozens of boulders, but they all looked the same from this new angle.

They all looked the same.

A chill of fear swept over him. Where was their trail? Which way had they come up? He felt the wind lift his hair.

Meato peered up the cliff, looking for cairns or any sign of Ideth and the cave.

"How could she do this to me?" he fumed.

But then he remembered something and relaxed. He'd played this game before a million times with his parents. They'd get all tough about something and threaten to make him "live with the consequences," but they always rescued him in the end. Just last month, he'd forgotten his homework, and when his mother had dropped him off at school, she'd been very upset with him.

"This is what happens when you don't take responsibility," she'd chided him in an ominous tone. "Your teacher is going to be very disappointed and make you stay after school to finish."

But by the time classes started, his Mother had scooted home, retrieved his homework, and dropped it off at his school.

"Ideth will be back," Meato reassured himself smugly. And then he said out loud, in a mocking tone: "Am I right, or am I right?"

He was wrong.

While Meato sat in the warm sun on the side of the cliff, waiting for Ideth to save him, Ideth was busy fashioning a broom out of Krog Pad willow branches while her chowder simmered to perfection.

"I'd forgotten they have such good clams here," she thought hungrily, as she inhaled some of the heavenly fumes up her wide-open nostrils.

Meanwhile, Meato happily entertained himself by exploring the ground beneath his feet, spending a full hour watching some busy ants remove a twig from the entrance to their hole. But by the time the sun had passed the zenith and was approaching the western horizon, he suddenly felt all alone. And terribly hungry, too. The wind had died down and it was quiet and still. A lizard peeked out from under a boulder.

She's not coming, buddy! it seemed to say. *You're on your own!*

"She's not coming," Meato realized, with a feeling that was part awe and part terror. He couldn't believe it, but there it was. *She wouldn't be coming to rescue him.* He'd be spending the night on the side of the bluff, without Ideth, his ducky sack, or any food. It took a moment for the truth to truly sink in.

And then he began to cry.

Some people think that crying is a sign of weakness, but it's not. People cry when they lose someone they love, for example, and it's a healthy part of the grieving process. But people also cry when they stumble on an uncomfortable truth, one of the harsh facts of life that they can't escape. And in Meato's case, he was facing up to the fact that everyone is ultimately responsible for themselves. He hadn't learned this from his parents, because they always stepped in and protected him. But Ideth wasn't going to do that, and it was up to him to get out of the pickle he'd gotten himself into. He was going to have to find Ideth's trail and climb it, or go hungry and sleep on rocks.

When Meato was all cried out (it took a good ten minutes) and all that was left were hiccups, he wiped his face with the hem of his loincloth and began picking his way upward. His hands were trembling and his mouth went dry with fear, but he kept going. And after searching for a few minutes, to his great relief, he finally saw a cairn, and then another and another, marking a trail that climbed steeply but not so severe that he couldn't navigate it.

It took him more than an hour, and he had to stop often to catch his breath. He didn't dare look down, for when he did, his legs began scissoring and he felt a wave of nausea pass through him. But just before sunset, he finally saw the mouth to Ideth's cave, which she had marked with a Krog Pad willow broom.

When he appeared at the entrance and looked inside, Ideth was busy puttering about. But she looked up when he said a weary "hello."

"Ah ha! There you are," she said. "I hoped you make it before dark. Now doesn't this chowder smell divine?"

"And hot Win-Nin too, right?" asked Meato. Hot chocolate was one of his favorite comfort foods and the image of a steaming cup had been a strong motivator for helping him climb the bluff.

"As promised," replied Ideth. "I've been drying the beans ever since we arrived. They're good and ready."

When dinner was over and Meato was so stuffed that he could barely move, Ideth cleaned up the dishes, throwing him a dish towel to help dry, which he did without thinking.

"Now come over here and let me show you something," Ideth said afterwards. "I found some glass jars up here and I want to prepare some pickled herring. Another uppy must have used this cave, because these jars aren't mine. But since they're here, I can show you how to make your own food. Then you can eat whatever you want, wherever you go, without relying on anyone else. There's great freedom in that, especially for foodies like us."

This idea appealed to Meato. If he could make his own food, anywhere and anytime, it meant he'd never go hungry again.

It was hard for him to remember how hungry he'd been only a couple of hours before, struggling up the bluff. But even though he was stuffed now, the experience had gotten his full attention. He couldn't rely on Ideth to take care of him, he could see that now. It would be far better to learn to make his own food than rely on her or anyone else. So he watched and listened with interest over the next hour as she showed him how to pickle.

"That was pretty easy," said Meato when they were done.

"I know what you mean," replied Ideth. "New things are never as scary as you think they're going to be. I didn't start cliff-diving until last year. I was the oldest person in the training class, but I didn't care. It's always good to push yourself, that's what I say. And besides, cliff-diving doesn't require special clothes or a lot of expensive equipment. It's just you, gloriously naked, and the ocean hundreds of feet below. Perhaps I can show you how to do it while you're here."

Meato gulped. Paddling had been scary enough. He imagined himself diving off a cliff and missing, hitting the beach instead and breaking open his skull, his brains smashed to smithereens.

"Oh, all right," Ideth clucked with a smile. "We'll just stick to cooking. You can't crack your head open doing that, can you?"

Chapter 15

A BREAK IN THE CASE

"Yup! We've arrested someone," Officer Joshua Morgan told Mateo's parents. He was standing in their living room, looking triumphant.

"Oh, my goodness," Mateo's mother whispered, slumping against her husband.

It had been three weeks and there hadn't been any leads in the case. Now the police had arrested someone and maybe they'd find out what had happened to Mateo. Maybe they'd get him back at last.

"The suspect's denying any involvement," Officer Morgan continued, "but remember that bloody dish towel we found in your kitchen? I thought it might be Mateo's blood, but it's not. It came from the man you hired to fix your roof. From Bob's Roofing. Do you remember him?"

"Yes," Evelyn said tentatively, a confused look on her face.

Before she could say any more, Officer Morgan's cell phone began ringing the theme to Star Wars, and he held up a finger to silence her while he took the call.

"Yup, yup! I see," he said, as he listened to the person on the other end of the line. "Well, what did they do with the body then? Is it in the morgue?"

"Is Mateo dead?" asked Roberto, stepping in front of his wife as if to protect her.

Evelyn breathed in sharply, her hand over her mouth. She'd been dreading this moment. If Mateo was dead, she didn't know whether life would be worth living. She'd have to live for Alex, she knew, but it would be terrible. And poor Mateo! He'd been such a wonderful boy, she realized. Not lazy at all. Just a child with a lively imagination who was happier than all of them put together. She just hadn't seen it.

"Another case," Officer Morgan mouthed at Roberto and Evelyn, to their enormous relief, before turning his attention back to his call.

He listened for another 30 seconds or so, clearly annoyed, and then barked, "Well if that's the kind of condition the body's in, I wonder why they even want to bury it!" Then he snapped the phone shut and turned back to face Mateo's parents, as if nothing had just happened.

"Now where were we?" he asked, scanning his memory. "Ah, yes. I was just about to tell you that we don't yet know where Mateo is, but we're hoping the suspect will tell us. Yup, yup! I can't make any promises, but we'll try to get to the bottom of what happened. Dead or alive, we'll do everything we can to find your son. At least we have a lead now. This late in the game, we often never find out what happened. Cases grow cold and we have to move on. It's a fact of this job."

He pulled out a pad of paper and began scribbling.

"Grocery list," he smiled apologetically. "If I don't write things down when they enter my mind, I forget about them. Drives my wife crazy."

Roberto and Evelyn looked at each other, their eyebrows furrowed in anger. Officer Morgan was making a grocery list while their son was missing and might still be alive and waiting to be rescued! How could he be so relaxed at a time like this? He needed to be doing something.

"I remember the roofer," Evelyn said, trying to move the investigation forward. "His name was Jimmy Albini. He was such a nice man! He was the only one who could find the leak above Mateo's bedroom. We'd tried three other roofers before we found him. He was going to come back to finish the work, to seal up the hole so it wouldn't leak anymore. But then Mateo went missing and I told him his work would have to wait. I can't believe it!"

"It often happens that way," said Officer Morgan grimly. "Yup! The man comes to work at the home. Sees the kid. Comes back later and snatches him. Then the kid is dead within a matter of hours. These criminals like to cover their tracks. Usually get rid of the body down a mineshaft or some such. If we're lucky, we might find Mateo's bones."

Evelyn dissolved in tears.

"Enough!" cried Roberto. "I appreciate you keeping us informed, Officer Morgan, but I will not have you upsetting my wife. She's not up to this. You're the most insensitive person I've ever met."

Officer Morgan was taken aback. He thought he was being helpful. But he could see that he'd just made matters worse. He apologized and left rather abruptly, but before he went, he assured Roberto and Evelyn that he would stay in touch.

"I'll call you with more details as I get them. You'll be the first to know. Yup! Definitely before the press does anyhow."

Mateo's parents sat down on the couch in their living room. Evelyn was shaking. The fine house by the sea glinted in the sun.

"At least they have a lead," she whispered, in a resigned tone. "Surely we can't expect any other kind of good news at this point."

Later that evening, Roberto's cell phone rang and he took the call.

"I just got off the phone with the crime lab," reported Officer Morgan briskly. "Yup! They got a hit on CODIS, the national DNA database. That's how they figured out that it was Albini's blood on the dish towel. And then they found out from his boss that he'd worked at your house. He was there the very day Mateo disappeared. They've nabbed the right guy, all right. And he's got a rap sheet that'll make you want to weep."

"We're weeping already, I can assure you," Roberto replied, coldly. He couldn't believe how blasé Officer Morgan was being about the whole affair. "If you were a doctor you'd tell your patient 'Yup! Yup! You're dying of heart disease! You can't expect to live much longer now. You'd better choose a tombstone.'"

There was a pause on the line and Roberto could hear the sound of someone, probably Officer Morgan, typing on a keyboard. The man wasn't even listening.

And it was true. Officer Morgan didn't know what to do with himself if he wasn't multi-tasking. He had to keep busy to avoid facing how dismal and disappointing his life had become. It wasn't at all the way he'd envisioned it when he was a boy. Back in first grade, he'd told everyone he wanted to be a policeman and puffed out his tiny little chest with pride. Now he wished he'd known what he was getting into. No one liked having to tell the parents of a missing child that the kid was probably dead and they might never find him, even his bones. What a terrible job he had, especially at times like this.

"Well, I just thought you should know the way the winds are blowing," Officer Morgan said, his hands poised over his keyboard in mid-sentence. He was typing up a report that was a week overdue and he needed to get it done or there'd be big trouble.

"Please keep us updated," Roberto said, annoyed but not wanting to alienate Officer Morgan by showing his anger and impatience.

"Yes, I assure you I will. Because there's nothing as terrible as *not knowing what happened*, is there?"

Then Officer Morgan snapped shut his cell phone, leaving Roberto with his mouth open, appalled that Officer Morgan had been assigned to Mateo's case and hoping against hope that Mateo would be found safe and alive despite the policeman's apparent indifference.

IKTAE

After the day on the bluffs, life fell into a happy routine for Ideth and Meato. Meato usually slept in the cave, for navigating down the bluff after dinner was dangerous. In the mornings, Ideth woke early, puttering in her hush-hush way that made her lovable, but drove him crazy. He woke, fell asleep, woke again, fell asleep, woke again, fell asleep, and then finally woke up for good with a sigh. Then they made breakfast together. When Ideth did the cooking, Meato cleaned up, and when Meato did the cooking, Ideth cleaned up.

If someone had visited Mateo's house for dinner in Monterey, where he slunk around just out of reach to avoid being asked to help, they would have been astonished at the change. Meato was a different Mateo. He chipped in without being asked because he actually enjoyed it. Ideth didn't force him to do it, which made a big difference. She didn't nag him or make threats she didn't plan to follow through on. She didn't compare him to anyone else. And she liked his sense of humor.

Sometimes he'd goof around with Ideth when they were working together and she always joined in the fun. One morning, for example, while he was drying one of her precious delicate plates, he cried "Oops!!" and pretended to drop it. The horrified look on Ideth's face sent him into peals of laughter. When she realized he was joking, she chased him around the cave with her broom until they were both out of breath and fell to the floor, tears of mirth spilling out of their eyes.

"I was thinking maybe Shum and I could play bluff Frisbee with it," Meato grinned.

"Not a chance," replied Ideth, still laughing. "My grandmother gave me those plates and if you break them I'll skin your hide."

After breakfast, Meato usually practiced his climbing skills for an hour or two. Ideth called it "risk training," and he was getting highly skilled. The trail from the beach to the cave was easy for him now, and he could ascend it in less than nine minutes, four times faster than Ideth's best record. His feet had grown tough with calluses, too, and he preferred going barefoot. Sometimes he climbed all morning, exploring the upper reaches of the bluffs, without a trace of fear. Then, the rest of the day he would spend on the beach and at sea, playing delightful, imaginative games with his duppies—and reading.

Shum, it turned out, had a daughter, a wide-eyed little girl named Iktae, who was unusually shy for a Krog Padder. Somehow, she'd gotten ahold of a book, which she carried around with her like a sodden doll. It was an unusual toy to have on Krog Pad, an island that had no schools, no libraries, and no buildings of any kind. So Meato was curious to know where she'd found it.

"Come with me!" she whispered to Meato when he asked her about it. She took him by the hand and led him to an area at the foot of the bluffs that was partly covered by brush. Meato could see the remains of a wrecked boat sticking out of the sand.

"Come from sea!" she said pointing to the boat and then back to her book.

Meato raised his eyebrows in understanding.

"Books good be!" he said, speaking in the choppy Krog Pad dialect he'd grown so fond of.

"Other worlds see?" Iktae asked hopefully, handing him the book. "You read me?"

Meato fingered the pages doubtfully. The book was soggy and the pages were matted together. The back cover was missing altogether and the binding was beginning to come apart. He flipped it over and could just see the title: *Insurance Law: Cairntip Province.*

"I'll have to see what Ideth has," he thought. "I can't turn Iktae off to reading with a snoozer like this."

Fortunately, Ideth had brought two good books and was willing to let Meato borrow them.

"Don't let the Krog Padders get them," she warned. "They're likely to rip them up just to sharpen their teeth."

Meato didn't tell her that he was planning to read them to Iktae, but Ideth knew.

"He's a sweet boy," she thought affectionately, "and goodness knows the Krog Padders need at least one good reader among them. There's certainly no harm in it."

And so the reading lessons began. Every day after lunch, when the Krog Padders flopped for an hour or so, Meato and Iktae ran off together, to the rowboat, and Meato read to her. He started with *The Good Urth*, a cookbook with sample recipes from nearly every island on Urth. "Cairntip Deep Dish Salmon-Potato Pie," "Grilled Amdar Halibut with Chilled Lemon-Hazelnut Sauce," "Spicy Wannabe Shrimp and Conch Pasta."

Recipes from Krog Pad Island and Finding Island, however, were notably absent.

"There is no culinary culture on Krog Pad," the author wrote, dismissively. For Finding Island, she referred her readers to a companion book: *Surviving a Finding: Fruit, Fruit, and More Fruit*, calling it "the definitive work on the topic."

Meato tried to teach Iktae to read straight away, but she was a slow learner. She didn't even know how real language sounded. So Meato began reading to her, and even talking to her, just like he talked to Ideth and his friends and family back home in Monterey. As the limited Krog Pad vocabulary and excessive exclamation points dropped away, replaced by colorful, musical language, Iktae entered a culinary universe so dazzling that sometimes she fell mute. And she also felt bonded to Meato in a very special way. She thought he was the most wonderful, brilliant, amazing big brother a girl could have, and she followed him around like a puppy.

"How is Iktae's reading coming along?" asked Ideth one evening after dinner.

"I figured you knew I was teaching her to read," Meato smiled. "We're done with *The Good Urth* and we've just started *Tales by Moons-Light: Stories from Before the Great Melt*. I drew a picture of us reading on the beach together."

Ideth looked at the sketch and smiled approvingly.

"It's a nice likeness of both of you," she praised. "And I'm so glad that I can get *The Good Urth* back now. I have lots of recipes I want to try. When can I have it? Before tomorrow's dinner, I hope?"

She couldn't wait to get her hands on the book again.

There was a silence, followed by another silence, and then a third, even longer one.

"I'm really, *really* sorry, Ideth," Meato finally said, with an embarrassed grimace. "Shum got it. There was nothing I could do."

Ideth sighed. She'd been afraid of this. The last time she'd been on Krog Pad, one of the Krog Padders had gotten into her buoy before she'd been able to unload it and hide everything away in a cave, where it would have been safe. Every scrap of food had been pilfered and all her books had been torn to shreds. Krog Padders loved to chew on anything they could get their hands on. And books were simply too irresistible to them.

"Not that they even *try* to control themselves," she stewed. "They just do whatever makes them happy without giving any thought to others. So self-centered."

"Did he destroy the *whole* thing?" she asked with an inkling of hope. Perhaps she could rescue some recipes.

"I'm afraid so. He ripped it up and ran into the ocean with it. Then he and some of the others tossed it about until it sank. I watched them do it and pleaded with them to stop, but they were so happy that I couldn't get too upset with them. They were having so much fun."

"Humph!" replied Ideth with annoyance. "That's typical. We enjoy watching them have fun and let them get away with all kinds of mischief. Well, I'll just have to stick to the recipes that I have stored in my memory. But it's such a shame. Some of the Amdar recipes are so creative. They put ingredients together that you never dreamed could taste so delicious. The Southern Islands are famous for their cuisine. I wish I could take you there, but it can't be helped. If you had the gift of *Feeling Deeply* it would different. Then you could cruise to Amdar with your uppy and feast at every meal. There are formal dinners on cruises. It's a bunch of nonsense if you

ask me. It's the food I'd want, not all the linen tablecloths, silver serving bowls, and obsequious waiters."

"What's obsequious?" asked Meato.

"Never you mind. It's all very ridiculous and plenty of fuss and bother. Meanwhile, here I am on Krog Pad without a proper cookbook."

"That's okay," said Meato. "I wrote down some of the best recipes in my sketch pad so Iktae could see me write. I can't believe the Krog Padders don't teach their children to read and write. Only Iktae seems to care about it."

"Iktae is unusual," Ideth agreed, "and I'd like to think that she'll grow up into an educated woman who can get off Krog Pad someday."

"Yes," agreed Meato. "Maybe she could even go to college."

Ideth's face darkened. There was little chance that Iktae would ever go to college. She'd be lucky to live long enough to have children of her own. But she didn't have the heart to tell Meato why. At least not yet.

"I think Iktae has already renamed herself," Meato told her later as they warmed their toes together by the fire. "Her birth name was Katie. But she seems too young for renaming. She's only five in earth years."

"The children of Krog Pad rename themselves earlier than children on other islands," replied Ideth, closing her eyes wearily. It had been a long day and the topic of conversation was not one she wanted to pursue.

"Why?"

"Oh, I don't know," muttered Ideth, though she knew she was being dishonest. "Now, let's go to bed so we can wake up early. I want to try one of those recipes you copied from *The Good Urth*. The bluffberries are getting ripe and there's nothing better than a fresh bluffberry pie for breakfast."

"Okay," Meato agreed, dropping the subject of Iktae. But as he laid out his ducky sack and crawled inside, he was troubled by Ideth's unwillingness to discuss her.

He would dream about Iktae, he knew. She was always in his dreams now, carrying around her soggy book and looking to him for help. And he liked it. It made him feel important and needed in a way that he'd never felt back home in Monterey. Not even Vortex looked up to him like that, probably because he often forgot to feed him.

Vortex's sad eyes entered his mind, staring at him through the patio door, his empty food dish at his feet.

"Poor dog," he thought guiltily. "If I ever get home, I'll never neglect Vortex again, just like I'll never neglect Iktae."

It gave him great joy to imagine sneaking Iktae a slice of Ideth's bluffberry pie. They would share it in their little retreat in the bushes by the boat and read *Tales by Moons-Light: Stories from Before the Great Melt*, licking the red berries off their fingers, being careful to hide away the book afterwards, under the boat, where it was safe. Iktae was the only Krog Padder he could trust not to destroy it. For some odd reason, she understood the power of books, even before anyone had read one to her. She would never grab it in her mouth and run down the beach with it, wildly happy, tearing it apart as she went.

No, Iktae wasn't like her parents or the other residents of Krog Pad Island, just like Ideth had told him. But there had been something very sad in the way she'd refused to discuss Iktae's renaming. And as he continued to contemplate this as he drifted off to sleep, a little hole opened up inside him, deep in his belly where fear comes from, and he tossed and turned all night in restless confusion.

Chapter 17

NEAP TIDES

"**M**y duppies are hungry!" shouted Meato, running into the cave, where Ideth was mending his shirt.

Ideth looked up. Meato looked tanned and fit in his loincloth. He had real climbing muscles now.

"Of course they are," she said, barely looking up from her work. "The neap tides have come. There'll be very little pickings on the beach for a while."

Meato frowned. "What do you mean?"

"The pulls of Lunera, Ru, and the sun have evened out," she said. "The tides will stand still for a few days. No tides bringing the food in, and no tides taking the water out."

"But what will they eat if they can't go beachcombing?"

"Nothing much," she replied, matter-of-factly.

Meato was appalled. These were his friends, Shum's people. His duppies. He couldn't let them go hungry.

"Ideth, they're all moping about on the beach crying 'Poor we! Hungry be! No food! No food see!' I've never seen them like this. It's heartbreaking!" he exclaimed.

"Ha!" replied Ideth, pursing her lips. "Well, it serves them right. They don't harvest more food than they need when the pickings are abundant. They just leave the leftovers and let the tides take them away. Now they have nothing saved up and I'm supposed to feel sorry for them? I don't think so. They made their own bed, now they can lie in it."

"Well, I don't care *what* you say, Ideth," Meato exclaimed, stamping his foot. "There must be something we can do to help them. We have extra food, a whole cave full of it," he argued. "We've been pickling and drying food since the first week. Can't we share some of it with them, just to get them through?"

Ideth turned her head and looked directly into his eyes, one brow raised.

"It seems to me," she said, "that the Krog Padders are responsible for themselves. If they were disabled or weak or incapable in some way, I'd have sympathy. But there's nothing wrong with them. If you feed them, you're just enabling them to remain this way. I know it seems harsh, but that's how it is. They'll not be getting any of our food and, fortunately, they can't raid our stocks because they can't climb up here."

Meato slumped to the floor by the front door of the cave.

"I can't stand watching them. I had a conch burger in my pocket and they could all smell it. They stood around me in a circle, with their eyes fixed on it. And then they began to sniff the air, their noses twitching. I tore up my burger into small pieces and shared it around, but no one got very much. When I started back for the cliff, they followed me all the way to the beginning of the trail and began to howl with misery: 'Meato see! We no happy be!' Give food to we!' I told them I'd see what I could do."

Meato looked out over the lip of the cave to the beach below. He couldn't quite see the Krog Padders because they were huddled right at the bottom of the trail, where he'd left them, and out of sight. But he could hear their wails over the slosh of the distant surf.

"Big bunch of overgrown babies," said Ideth with disgust. "They'll be hungry for a few days and then they'll forget all about it. As soon as the tides shift, they'll get busy eating again and start shouting 'Happy be!' You just wait and see. But we'll not be going hungry thanks to your industry. Your pickled herring is spectacular."

Meato went inside the cave to escape from having to listen to the Krog Padders. He knew he wouldn't be able to eat while they went hungry. He couldn't understand how Ideth could just sit there, slurping up pickled herring, when she knew what was happening on the beach.

"I'll go on a hunger strike," he thought. "Maybe that will change Ideth's mind."

Meato started his hunger strike immediately after lunch. (If you ever decide to go on a hunger strike, you'll find that it's easier to start right after a big meal.) Then he broke the strike for dinner because Ideth made conch fries, his favorite. I have to give Meato some much-deserved credit here, for he managed to skip both breakfast and lunch the following day, without sneaking anything behind Ideth's back. But by dinnertime, he'd lost his will power again and was beginning to side with Ideth about the whole affair.

"You're sure they'll be back to normal in a few days?" asked Meato. "I miss them!"

"Like clockwork," she said. "You'll see. For the time being, though, you'd better stay up here. They'll follow you around begging if you don't."

Meato knew it was impossible to keep secrets from Ideth, but he began to hatch a plan anyway. Shum and his like could starve for a few days, he decided, but he wasn't going to let it happen to Iktae.

"I need to get something to her," he thought. "And I need to do it while Ideth's asleep because I don't think she can read my mind then."

He paused. Could Ideth be reading his mind now? What if she was eavesdropping in and knew all about what he was planning to do? He didn't know, but he decided to risk it. The worst she could do was stop him and the best he could do was get away with it.

After a dinner of dried octopus with lime sauce, which sounded awful to Meato but was actually quite tasty, Meato eyed Ideth closely. She returned to her mending, but she gave up trying to fix his shirt because she'd misplaced her glasses again and couldn't thread the needle. So she crawled into her ducky sack and said goodnight.

"I hope he doesn't trip on the trail in the dark, poor thing," she thought as she closed her eyes. She knew exactly what Meato was going to do.

Meato, not knowing that Ideth knew what he was afraid she might know, tiptoed out of the cave. He'd managed to slip a

packet of dried limes and a bottle of pickled herring into Ideth's backpack, which he'd borrowed for the purpose. Ru was up, but Meato was accustomed to climbing the bluffs in broad daylight, not at night. Fortunately, he knew the route practically by heart now. Holding onto rocks for support as he found them, and keeping an eye out for landmarks, he groped his way down. Twice he got lost and had to backtrack, but he finally reached the beach. It had probably taken him no more than half an hour but he was sure it must have been three.

Meato knew where his duppies would be flopped. It was the same place they slept every night. And he knew each one of them by name now—there were about 60 in all. When Meato had first met the Krog Padders, they'd all looked pretty much alike, but when he began to spend time with them, he picked up on subtle differences. Within a few days, he could easily tell them apart. If you regularly visit a zoo (which I hope you do because it's loads of fun), the same will happen there. The lions will all look the same at first, but pretty soon you'll be calling the female one with the short tail Sally and the male one with the black mane Frank. That's just how it goes.

Meato reached Dubdy first. He had an extra toe on his left foot and was the fastest paddler among them. He was curled up into a pathetic little ball, sleeping through his misery. Then Meato stumbled on Saidy, who was plumper than the others. Her nose was wiggling and her eyelids were twitching, making it clear she was dreaming about food.

Meato wandered through the sleeping forms until he found Iktae, lying beside Shum. Her mother was on the other side, a protective arm resting across her daughter's back.

"I need to get her away from everyone else before I try to wake her," he thought. "If I wake up any of the others, they'll see I have food. It's not even worth contemplating what that would be like."

Meato gently shifted Iktae's sleeping body so he could slide her out from between her parents. Then he carried her tiny form out to an area of soft beach grass, well away from the others.

"Wake up, Iktae," Meato whispered in her ear. "I have food!"

Iktae remained limp in his arms.

"*Food!*" he whispered again, a little louder, shaking her gently.

This time she heard him, and her beautiful, quiet eyes opened.

"You like prince be," she said softly, sleepily reaching up to hug him.

"I have some dried limes and pickled herring," he told her proudly. "I made the herring myself."

Iktae sat up slowly, for she was quite weak from lack of food now. As Meato pulled the bottle from the backpack and opened the lid, she became excited.

"Good be!" she said, when Meato fed her some. She ate it with such relish that it made him want to cry.

"You mustn't tell anyone else about this," Meato warned her after she was done eating, "or there will be trouble tomorrow. It's only a few more days until the tides return, but I'll come down from the bluffs every night to feed you. I won't come down during the day, though. It's too hard on me to watch you guys suffer like this when we have food up there in the cave. It's too hard on me, Iktae. I hope everyone will understand."

Iktae nodded, solemnly.

"Listen to me," he said, looking her straight in the eyes. "It's complete nonsense to go through these famines. You don't have to. You could harvest more than you need during the syzygies and trilogies and then save it for the neaps. It's such a simple idea. Ideth can give you recipes for pickling and drying so the food will keep, and I can teach you."

Iktae beamed. "*Good Urth,*" she said.

"Yes," Meato whispered.

There was an awkward pause.

"Daddy be sorry he took the book," said Iktae, staring down at her hands. "Shame after. Cry even."

"I know, I know," replied Meato with a little laugh. "But I wrote down some of the recipes in my sketch pad, remember? So we haven't lost everything."

"Writing good?" asked Iktae.

"Yes," he affirmed. "If you write things down, you have them forever."

After a few more minutes, Meato returned Iktae to her sleeping parents. "Remember, I'll come every night," he whispered. And then he left her.

It was difficult sneaking food out of the cave the following few evenings after Ideth went to bed. A couple of times he was sure that Ideth would wake up and stop him, but she never did. His trips down the bluffs were hazardous and he slipped several times, giving himself some nasty scrapes. But he was faithful to Iktae, and she ate every night, no matter what.

Slowly the tides began to return. Then one morning, as he was high on the bluffs climbing, he looked down on the beach and saw that life was back to normal. Shum and his buddies were running joyously up and down the beach and leaping in the waves. That night, Meato got his first decent night's sleep in four days.

As he and Ideth crawled into their ducky sacks, she turned to him with a smile.

"Well done, findling," she said.

"What do you mean?" asked Meato.

"I think you know," replied Ideth.

"I couldn't let her go hungry," Meato said simply. "No matter what you said. She's my little sister now."

"Yes," said Ideth, a lump in her throat. "And you're a good big brother to her."

"I'm so glad the tides have come back," Meato said. "Now everything will be okay."

"Well," Ideth replied slowly. "At least they'll have plenty to eat for a while. That's something I guess."

"It's everything!" Meato responded brightly. "Now things will be back to normal, won't they?"

But he knew that something was wrong. There was a sadness in Ideth's tone that told him that. She was keeping something from him. He'd sensed it ever since she'd refused to discuss Iktae's renaming.

"Iktae's becoming a good reader," he said, hoping, somehow, that this would get life back on track.

"Yes," Ideth said, patting his hand with hers. "Thanks to you. And who knows? Maybe Iktae will write a book about Krog Pad one day. Wouldn't that be nice?"

It would be a miracle, she knew, but stranger things had happened. Where there was life, there was always hope.

"Yes," said Meato. "She'll get into a good college on Cairntip. I know it. She's already beginning to speak normally and she can do some simple math, too."

"Well, that's fine," replied Ideth as she turned off her hurricane lamp and eased over on her side. "Now let's get some sleep. The weather is beginning to turn. We're well into the monsoon season now and it's high time for some bad weather. There were dark clouds in the west this evening. Did you notice them? It might mean rain. And though this cave won't flood, it will get mighty wet if we don't cover the fissure properly. I'll show you how to do it if it comes to that. We wouldn't want all our supplies washing away, would we?"

Chapter 18

THE TRIAL OF J. O. ALBINI

"**I**s there DNA evidence in this case?" a grim-faced prosecutor asked his star witness, a petite criminalist named Stella Knight, who wore prim glasses and kept referring to a large, intimidating-looking binder.

The courtroom was packed. Mateo's parents sat near the front, holding hands. It had been nearly five months since Mateo had gone missing, and now it was time for justice. They stared angrily at the back of J. O. Albini's slightly balding head. He was dressed in a loose-fitting orange prison outfit and kept staring worriedly at his feet.

"There certainly is," Stella answered, swinging a pair of accusing eyes in the direction of the suspect. She'd worked closely with the prosecutor for many weeks and they'd practiced her testimony so it was carefully choreographed for maximum effect before she even took the stand.

"You found it on a dish towel in the Marino's kitchen, didn't you?"

"Yes," Stella affirmed. "There was blood on the towel and we got a full DNA profile from it."

She didn't move her eyes from J. O. Albini, who slumped even further in his chair. He was scared of women—*all* women—and the criminalist was more terrifying than most.

The prosecutor nodded grimly.

"So what you're saying is that Mr. Albini was in the Marino's kitchen on the day that Mateo was murdered?"

"That's right," she agreed, half-closing her eyes in smug scientific certainty. "His blood was all over it. He must have cut himself while knifing Mateo to death. That's what must have happened. Mr. Albini is as guilty as sin. Just look at him!"

The judge put up a finger to stop the prosecutor from asking any more questions. He was waiting for J. O. Albini's defense attorney to speak up.

"Do you wish to interject something here, Mr. Slepe?" prompted the judge. "Perhaps you'd like to object? After all, Miss Knight wasn't there. How can she possibly know how Mr. Albini's blood got on the towel? How do we even know that Mateo was murdered? We don't have a body, do we?"

The judge knew full well that August Slepe should object. Any competent attorney wouldn't let a witness get away with such wild speculations.

But this wasn't the first time he'd presided over a trial where August Slepe was the defense attorney, and he knew that Slepe often snoozed when he should have been defending. The man should never have been awarded a law degree and now it was too late. It was a very, very sad situation for Slepe's client, Jimmy Albini. Very sad. It was clear the poor man wasn't a child

killer. He'd seen a few child killers in his career and he could tell that Jimmy was not one of them.

"Objection!" responded August Slepe groggily, his eyes half shut.

"Sustained!" barked the judge in relief. Then he turned to the prosecutor. "The jury decides whether Mr. Albini is guilty of murder, Mr. Thomas, not you and Miss Knight. Stick to the facts."

The prosecutor let out a loud "humph" and rolled his eyes at the jury, but he obediently changed his line of questioning.

"I see on page 43 of your report, Miss Knight, that you compared the DNA profile found on the bloody towel with Mr. Albini's DNA profile and it matched perfectly. Will you please read your conclusion to the jury, just as it's written in your report?"

"Of course," replied Stella, adjusting her glasses. "The DNA profile obtained from the blood on the towel is the same as Mr. Albini's. The chance that it's *not* Mr. Albini's blood is one in a quadrillion billion."

"Wow!" cried the prosecutor, as if he'd never discussed this finding with Stella and was shocked at the strength of the evidence. "That's incredible!"

Stella turned to the next page of her report and scanned it for another incriminating passage.

"It's a scientific certainty that Mr. Albini murdered Mateo," Stella read. "It's the opinion of this crime lab that he's guilty of murder."

August Slepe appeared to be doodling, and the judge stepped in yet again.

"Mr. Slepe! This is another opportunity to object! Wake up! How can Miss Knight know that Mr. Albini's blood got on the towel during a *murder*? We don't even know that Mateo has been killed!"

Mr. Slepe's pencil stopped moving and he looked up, adjusting his glasses as if he'd just realized he was in a courtroom.

"Objection, your Honor!"

"On what grounds?" the judge said, encouragingly, hoping against hope that Mr. Slepe had been listening to what he'd just said and would repeat it back to the court.

"Not sure," said Mr. Slepe, rubbing his forehead in confusion.

The judge sighed.

"Overruled," he said in disgust. "You should have paid attention in law school, Mr. Slepe. I feel sorry for your poor client, that's all I have to say."

The prosecutor, who was having an excellent day, flourished through his notes, creating a dramatic effect.

"Well, I think we all know by now that there was a murder and who committed it," he said, turning to the jury box. "I've never seen a guiltier suspect in all my life."

J. O. Albini winced and looked at Mr. Slepe, who (as you've probably guessed) had gone back to sleep. In fact, his chin was on his chest and he'd started snoring.

"I'm going to get convicted!" Jimmy thought in sudden certainty, the blood draining from his face. "He's not going to save me!"

"Mr. Slepe, it would be lovely if you could join us back here in the courtroom," the judge said sarcastically. "I think your client would appreciate it!"

"Objection!" Slepe cried, getting to his feet.

"Grounds?" asked the judge, once more hoping to jog Mr. Slepe's memories from law school.

"Uh…" muttered Slepe, looking from his client to the judge and back again to his client.

"Er…because it's time to go home or I'll be late for my dinner?" he asked hopefully.

"Overruled again!" shouted the judge, furious now and banging down his gavel so hard that everyone's ears rang. "You can't object because you're hungry for your dinner and want to go home!"

"It's all right, judge," the prosecutor smiled when the sound of the gavel had faded away. "Miss Knight has done an excellent job of informing the jury about who killed Mateo. No further questions."

The trial lasted two weeks and Mateo's parents attended every day. Witnesses for the prosecution came to the stand, one after another, where the prosecutor twisted their words without any objection from Mr. Slepe.

A forensic psychologist testified that the "child-killer's" profile was astonishingly close to Mr. Albini's.

"The perpetrator is a male between thirty and forty years old," he said, reading from his report. "He was abused in childhood, has a history of minor offenses, and works with his hands."

A frail elderly receptionist from Bob's Roofing, where J. O. Albini worked, gave her testimony reluctantly. She liked Jimmy Albini and didn't think he could do something as terrible as abducting and killing a child.

"Mrs. Wong," said the prosecutor, "on the morning of October 22nd, the day after Mateo Marino went missing, did Mr. Albini arrive at work on time?"

Mrs. Wong smiled. "Oh, yes! He was always on time and a real good worker."

She looked across at Jimmy and nodded at him in a motherly way.

"And on that day," the prosecutor said, "did your boss, Bob Grebes, send him home?"

"Well, yes ... yes, he did. But not because Jimmy did anything wrong. Jimmy has always been a good employee. No,

it was because his thumb was banged up and it wasn't safe for him to work that day."

"His thumb was cut?"

"Yes. He hurt it while working, and it was all wrapped up in gauze and tape."

"I see. Well, that's most unfortunate," said the prosecutor slyly.

"Yes, yes it was. You see, he was repairing the roof on the Marino's house. That's where he banged it up. Isn't that a shame?"

Mrs. Wong thought she was helping Jimmy Albini, but she suddenly realized that the prosecutor was going to use her words against him.

"He was working at the *Marino's* house?" the prosecutor asked, frowning. "The house of *Mateo Marino*, the murdered boy?"

"Well, yes, but Jimmy wouldn't hurt anyone."

"So you're asking this jury to believe that Jimmy Albini just happened to be at the Marino's house the day Mateo was abducted? And that he came to work the next day with a huge, bloody gash on his thumb? You think this was just an accident? A coincidence? *Really?*"

"Well," said Mrs. Wong, a bit confused now. She looked from the prosecutor to the jury and back again to Jimmy.

"Humph!" said the prosecutor. "I'm done with this witness!"

"Mr. Slepe," said the judge, "I assume you wish to cross-examine?"

"No questions," Mr. Slepe said, sleepily.

A few days later, the trial was over and August Slepe hadn't called a single witness to testify in his client's defense.

"Our side's case is so much stronger," Mateo's mother whispered to the prosecutor as final arguments concluded and the jury filed away.

The prosecutor sighed. "It is and it isn't," he explained. "The judge is right, we don't have a body, and it's very hard to get a murder conviction without one. But that defense attorney was a disaster, so we have a chance."

The jury deliberated for two long days. Mateo's parents, exhausted from the emotional drama of the trial and the past several months of agony over Mateo's loss, were unable to eat or sleep. But finally, they got the call.

"There's a verdict," the prosecutor told them. "It will be announced this afternoon."

The jury, poker-faced, filed into the jury box. Mateo's parents gripped each other's hands tightly, praying that they would get some closure, praying that justice would be served for Mateo, whom they were sure must be dead. For they surely and truly appreciated him now that he was gone and would have given anything—*anything*—to be able to tell him so.

"How do you find the defendant?" the judge asked the jury foreman.

"Guilty, your Honor," she said, staring straight at J. O. Albini, now a freshly convicted child killer, with one judgmental eyebrow raised.

"Thank God they got him," Roberto whispered as Evelyn broke down and wept in his arms.

It wasn't the outcome they'd been hoping for. They wanted Mateo to be alive. But they'd given up all hope now and they wanted his murderer to pay for his crime. And besides, it wiped away the *not knowing what happened*, which meant they could get on with their lives. They had to live for Alex now and let Mateo rest in peace. It was the only way they could keep moving from one miserable day to the next. The pain would never go away. Never. But it would be livable. They would survive.

Jimmy Albini began to tremble and tears sprang to his eyes. He'd been found guilty by a jury of his peers. *Guilty.* He looked over at August Slepe and shoved him gently on the shoulder.

"What happens now?" he whispered. "Will we appeal?"

"Appeal?" asked Mr. Slepe with a frown and a yawn.

"Yes, appeal!" Jimmy cried. "I didn't do it. I didn't murder Mateo. I told you that!"

Mr. Slepe looked at him and shook his head.

"If you kidnap and murder a child, Mr. Albini, you can't expect to get off. I hope they give you the death penalty for what you've done."

Then he shut his briefcase and left the courtroom while a guard put handcuffs on Jimmy. Work was over and it was time to wake up. After all, his dinner was waiting.

"My own attorney doesn't believe in my innocence," Jimmy Albini thought dejectedly. "If he doesn't, then nobody will."

And it was true. Everyone believed that Jimmy Albini was a child killer, except the judge, who looked down on him sorrowfully from his high bench and shook his head. He hated to see an injustice play out in his courtroom. It made him hate his job and wish he was a salesman at Motorcycle Dudes on Main Street or had some other job where lives weren't on the line.

And, of course, the judge was right. J. O. Albini was an innocent man. As the jury left the courtroom and a policeman hauled J. O. Albini away, Mateo was quite alive and healthier than ever. In fact, he had just finished reading *Tales by Moons-Light: Stories from Before the Great Melt* to Iktae and they were sharing a piece of Ideth's marvelous bluffberry pie under the bright Krog Pad sun.

Somehow, even though he was innocent, Jimmy Albini's blood had gotten onto a towel in the Marino's kitchen, and he was going to prison for it. But there was no family to help him, for he was alone in the world, which is very sad for anyone, but especially for someone like Jimmy. He was truly good at heart and would never have used a mouse trap to snare a mouse, much less abduct and kill a ten-year-old boy.

Jimmy had a history, you see, like everyone does, a story that was all his own. But his deadbeat attorney had never asked him about it because he'd simply assumed, from the day he'd met Jimmy, that his client was guilty. And though the jury never would have found Jimmy guilty if they'd known who he really was, they didn't know. So they went home to their families and got on with their lives, while Jimmy Albini was locked up and left to rot.

Chapter 19

AN INNOCENT MAN

J immy Oscar Albini had been raised by an angry, abusive stepfather and a mother who couldn't stay sober. He was a shy boy who'd been born with the gift of *Liking to Do Things Well*, but no one noticed. Unlike Mateo, he did not live in a fine house by the sea. He lived in a rundown part of town in a small apartment over a liquor store. His parents fed and clothed him, and they managed to get him to school most days, so no one knew what was happening, except the man who ran the store. He could hear the beatings, when Jimmy's stepfather got out his belt and whipped him across the buttocks.

Jimmy would cry out and his stepfather would say: "You're useless! You can't do anything well!" And because Jimmy liked to do things well, he began to feel very bad about himself.

Jimmy finished elementary school, just barely, and then joined a gang of local youths when he was 11. He had no other choice. The gang provided him protection and became his pseudo-family, replacing the one he'd never really had. What the gang did was mostly petty stuff—vandalism (which the gang leader called "playing jokes") and spraying graffiti on buildings and sidewalks ("playing tag"). But there was burglary, too.

Jimmy was scared of the gang leader, who called himself "King Pin," but he liked him too because King Pin recognized his gift.

"The kid has good hands," he'd say. "Always gets the job done well." King Pin became a father figure to Jimmy. King Pin was intimidating, but never beat him.

When Jimmy (AKA "Hands") was 14, the real problems began. One of his gang buddies ratted him out after a burglary. He never knew for sure who it was, but he suspected it was "Shrimp."

Shrimp could never keep his mouth shut and wound up in the "System" (short for the criminal justice system) before he was 13. After the burglary incident, Jimmy was in the System too, and he kept bouncing in and out of jail for the next five years. And every time he'd bounce in, the police would treat him like he was useless and couldn't do anything well. And every time he bounced out, no one would give him a job because he had a criminal record.

One night, while he was "out," he unwisely accepted a ride from some guys he didn't know very well.

"We're going to play golf Frisbee," they told him. "Why don't you come along?"

Jimmy didn't like the look of the driver, who was sleazy, even by Jimmy's low standards, but he decided to go with them anyway. A few minutes later, the driver sped through a red light, skidded across a parking lot, and collided with the brick wall of a police station. It was wicked bad luck for them to hit such a target, but once it had happened, there was nothing to be done. Jimmy and his "friends" were arrested and the car was searched

for drugs and alcohol. Sure enough, the cops found what they were looking for, and all of them were charged with possession of an illegal substance.

The charge didn't stick, at least for Jimmy, but it was an important moment for our story. The police took a cheek cell swab from him while he was in custody. The cops had his DNA and his profile was uploaded into CODIS, the national database, where the profiles of hardened criminals from all over the country are stored, along with those of misguided kids like Jimmy, who aren't hardened at all.

You can imagine that after this, Jimmy felt even worse about himself (as you would, too, if your DNA profile was in CODIS, which I hope it isn't). He wasn't a bad kid, even if he'd gotten into trouble. In fact, just like Mateo, he had a gift. But when everyone around you is telling you you're worthless, starting from the time you're very small, it becomes a part of who you are. You begin to feel that way about yourself inside, and then you don't need anyone else to convince you anymore.

When Jimmy was 19, though, he got a break. A judge put him in a special program designed to help young repeat offenders learn a trade. The boss of the construction company wasn't thrilled with taking him on, but he got some kind of compensation from the government that gave him an incentive. Jimmy's new boss was hard on him at first, but over time, he began to notice Jimmy's gift.

Jimmy was very careful in all his work and never left a nail sticking out or a leak unsealed. Eventually, the boss admired Jimmy's work so much that he decided to hire him as a permanent employee. Jimmy still didn't feel very good about himself, but at least he had a stable situation. After that, there were no more gang buddies or trips to jail. He'd survived a dead-end, dangerous life on the streets, and now he had a job and apartment of his own. He had a new and better life.

Jimmy had such a low opinion of himself that he didn't feel confident enough to ask a woman on a date. He rarely went out, except to go to work, and he kept to himself even there. He was a fine carpenter and eventually become an expert roofer. But he had almost no friends. In the evenings, he'd eat his microwaved dinners in front of his TV with his sole companion: a sorry-looking, multi-toed cat he called King Pin. He was a sad, lonely person who didn't feel worthy of the ratty little couch he sat on. But he was safe from the System. Blessedly safe.

Jimmy went along like this for several years, until he met Sarah, who worked at the deli down the block from his apartment. Sarah was fat and nice and very funny. She told him stories about growing up in a big, loving family. She had four sisters and no brothers and all her family members lived in town. They had big get-togethers at least once a month and celebrated each other's birthdays.

"When's your birthday, Jimmy?" she asked him one day, when he came in for a sandwich.

"January 11th," he told her. "But I never celebrate it."

"That's sad," she replied, looking at him with warm eyes. "Everyone deserves to have a birthday."

A few months later, Jimmy got up the courage to ask her to go to a movie with him.

She smiled and cocked her head to one side.

"You're a nice man, Jimmy," she said. "But I don't like you like that."

Jimmy slunk home and shut himself in his bathroom, looking into the mirror. "You're useless!" he shouted to his image. "You can't do anything well!"

It was only a week later that he was arrested for Mateo's abduction and murder, while he was carefully affixing tiles to the roof of a newly constructed tire store. He knew he hadn't done it, and he felt terrible for Mateo's parents when he found out what had happened. But because he felt so bad about himself, he didn't bother to look up the professional record of the public defender assigned to his case. He simply put his fate in Mr. Slepe's incapable hands and figured he probably deserved whatever he got. And, ultimately, that is why his deadbeat attorney, who graduated last in his class from a third-rate law school and doodled cartoons during court proceedings, took the easy way out. He didn't ask his client about the details of the days he spent working on the roof of the Marino's fine house by the sea. He just assumed that Jimmy was guilty and therefore wasn't worthy of his time and effort.

But Jimmy wasn't guilty, of course. Mateo wasn't dead; he was on Urth. No crime had been committed. Instead, Jimmy's blood got onto the towel in the Marino's kitchen in another way altogether, which August Slepe might have figured out if he'd been a decent attorney and cared more about his client than his dinner.

You see, there's something I haven't told you yet, something I skipped over way back at the beginning of this story. Just after Mateo had washed the lavender color off his fingers the day he went through the crack, Jimmy appeared at the front door, holding up his bleeding thumb.

"I've been working on your roof," he said, after knocking politely, "and I've cut myself. Could I trouble you to get me a bandage?"

It was a simple thing for Mateo to do and he even helped Jimmy wrap up his thumb. Then Jimmy left and Mateo returned to the kitchen, wiping his hands on a convenient towel before returning to his bedroom and the crack that awaited him there.

Bingo! The truth was as simple as that. Mateo had transferred some of Jimmy's blood onto the towel.

And now, perhaps, you'll be able to sleep at night, knowing what actually happened, unlike Jimmy, who slept on his dirty, sagging cot in prison listening to the obnoxious snoring of his cell mate, Big Bud, and writing love letters to Sarah in his mind.

Chapter 20

THE STORM

"**W**e're in for a massive storm," warned Ideth one morning, peering out of the cave, squinting at the sky. The monsoon season had swept in and they'd had squalls every day for several weeks. But the black, angry clouds that were gathered on the horizon this time were different. She knew they had only a few hours before the storm would hit.

"I love storms," Meato replied.

"I usually do, too. But this one's coming at a bad time. It's a trilogy, you know, and the tides will be wicked."

"But it's been a trilogy for a few days now," he pointed out. "And I like it. I've been sleeping with my duppies so I can star gaze with them. The Krog Padders have names for the constellations, and Iktae's been teaching them to me: *We See Three*, *Big Beast Be*, and *Like Seahorse Is*. They even have a name for the really bright star that we've been seeing in the west, right after sunset. They call it *Up Be?*"

"Humph," replied Ideth. "That's because it shifts between the morning and evening skies, like Venus does on Earth. They have no astronomy, so they have no way of predicting when it will appear. Ridiculous! The Krog Padders are so simple-minded. Their '*Up Be?*' is a planet, and its real name is Celestia. It's beautiful when seen through a proper telescope. It has three moons."

Meato pondered this. A planet with *three* moons! Wow! What would the tides be like there? And three moons in the sky? What would they call the moons-light when all three moons were up? *Moons-lights?* He imagined himself as Chief Astronomer on Celestia, draped in academic robes, poised at the eyepiece of a mighty telescope.

"This moon," he professed to an apprentice, "is Atome, this one is Matoe, and this one is Atemo. They were named after a god who prevailed over this planet before we all came into existence. He is a god who has three faces and wields a powerful sword called *Presence*." (He spelled 'presence' correctly this time, even in his head.)

"Please name one of the Moons Ethid," said Ideth, reading his mind. "After me. I only ask for one to be renamed after me. That's all. Am I right, or am I right?"

Meato headed down to the beach. The wind was up and he could smell rain. Dark gray clouds swelled on the western horizon and appeared to be moving in fast. The storm would be so exciting! His parents owned a vacation cottage in Mendocino, three hundred miles north of Monterey. When there, he liked nothing better than sneaking up to the third floor, under the eaves, to watch the rain whip sidewise onto the window glass. Sometimes he opened the window and hung his feet out, to feel the rain on his legs, as he did absolutely nothing, as usual. Or he might spin around the big globe up there and daydream about mysterious places to visit: Easter Island, the Marshall Islands, the Cayman Islands, Jamaica, Kenya, Norfolk Island, and impossibly distant and exotic Tasmania. Now, walking down to Krog Pad beach, he felt the same thrill and excitement. *A storm!* And he'd be lucky enough to be on Krog Pad Island during a trilogy to see it. It would be a whopper.

When he got down off the bluff and onto the beach, it was strangely empty. His duppies were nowhere to be seen. He walked down the beach to the boat wreck to look for Iktae, but she wasn't around either.

"What's going on with the Krog Padders today?" he wondered. "They're going to miss the fun of the storm!"

Meato wandered up the beach for about a mile in one direction, turned around, and then headed back.

He'd been walking with the wind behind him, he realized, because when he turned around, the strength of it caught him by surprise, blowing his hair back as far as it would go. Sand flew into his eyes and he had to squint and turn his head to the side to avoid it. And that's when he spotted the Krog Padders, standing side-by-side, in a long line, holding hands, facing the bluff.

Meato was stunned. He'd never seen the Krog Padders do this before and had no idea what it meant. Was it some kind of ritual? Goodness knows they had some weird beliefs, which he'd been able to figure out with the help of Iktae.

Gull fly! Sun sky! The Krog Padders were convinced that gulls brought up the sun in the morning. Meato had tried to explain the truth to Iktae, but talking about gravity and

Newton's Laws was difficult for him because he didn't really understand them himself.

Tide no! Fish go! They were certain, too, that all sea life disappeared during the neap tides. This was clearly ridiculous, and Iktae was amazed when Meato fashioned a simple fishing pole from a willow branch and a hook from Ideth's sewing kit. He baited it with some pickled herring, waded out into the surf, and had a fish flopping on the beach in less than 10 minutes.

"You could keep eating during the neap tides if you were just willing to work at it," he told Iktae. She looked at him like he was a wizard.

The Krog Padders also believed that when Lunera eclipsed Ru someone was going to die. (*Single moon! Die soon!*) Ideth explained to Meato that there were often moons-eclipses because the planer orbits of Lunera and Ru intersected.

"It's a lovely sight," she told him, with a shake of her head, "but it always has the Krog Padders in a frenzy. I have no idea how the belief got started. Probably one of their people died after a moons-eclipse. What nonsense!"

Meato made his way over to the Krog Padders and found Shum. He tugged on his arm. That's when he realized that Shum was shaking.

"SHUM! SHUM!" Meato shouted, over the sound of the wind. "LOOK AT ME! LOOK AT ME! WHY YOU NO HAPPY BE?"

Shum turned to him with a look of terror on his face.

"NO SEE! NOT BE!" he wailed, screwing his eyes tightly shut, as if he was in pain. Then he turned back toward the bluff.

"NO SEE, NOT BE!" wailed a woman further on down the line. Her eyes were squeezed shut, too, Meato noticed, as were the eyes of all the Krog Padders he could see nearby.

And then the chorus was taken up by others, up and down the line, in low male voices, higher women's voices, and the squeaky voices of their children: "NO SEE! NOT BE!"

A large cloud fell across the face of the sun, casting the beach into shadow.

"Iktae!" cried Meato, suddenly noticing her.

She was huddled in front of Shum, her arms locked around his knees in a violent embrace. She didn't answer.

"IKTAE!" he said louder to make his voice heard above the wind, kneeling down so he could talk directly to her. But she just shook her head and burrowed more fiercely against her father.

Meato didn't know what to think. He needed to ask Ideth what was happening. She would likely roll her eyes and tell him some ridiculous reason for this strange behavior. After the neap tides, it was hard to take anything the Krog Padders did with too much gravity. But he felt goose bumps on the back of his neck nonetheless.

Meato left his duppies and ran up the beach to get back to the trail to the cave. The lively feeling he'd had about the storm was turning to alarm. What did the Krog Padders' words mean? They had nothing to do with the moons, he was sure. They were in a trilogy, but the Krog Padders seemed to love lying on the beach under the wide sky and star gazing all night, a pleasure that was rare on a planet with two moons. Why had their behavior so suddenly changed?

When Meato reached the cave, he looked around for Ideth. She was probably out gathering Krog Pad acorns, which were ripe now. She'd told him she wanted to make Krog Pad acorn burgers for dinner that night.

"We'll be holed up here with the storm and all," she'd explained. "No star gazing tonight. I want to get all the cooking done in case the rain drowns the fire. I'll need you on hand to help."

Meato scanned the nearby bluffs and saw Ideth above him and in the distance. She was facing away from the ocean and leaning down, her backpack on one arm. Her hair was streaming in front of her in the wind, and he knew there was no way she could hear him. He climbed quickly up the bluff and approached her.

"MY DUPPIES ARE ACTING STRANGE!" he yelled loudly, over the wind. "THEY'RE STANDING IN A LINE, HOLDING HANDS, FACING THE BLUFF, AND SHOUTING 'NO SEE! NOT BE!' WHAT DOES IT MEAN? IT'S CREEPING ME OUT!"

Ideth looked up and gathered her hair in one hand to keep it under control.

"STORM AT TRILOGY!" she shouted back. "THIS TIME, THEIR FEAR IS WELL-FOUNDED!"

She pointed to the cave and looked at Meato with raised brows. He nodded, took the backpack, which was full of acorns,

and led the way down. Ideth needed one hand to hold her unruly hair and the other to steady her descent. The sky was completely covered with clouds by the time they made it back to the cave, and Meato thought he felt a raindrop land on his arm.

Ideth started a fire and then sighed.

"Sit down," she said. "This is a sad tale."

Meato sat, his feet straight out in front of him, facing the fire. He'd learned to keep his toes at just the right distance from the flames. Ideth sat beside him, poking at the fire with a stick.

"You know how the Krog Padders make no preparation for neap tides?" she began. "They just eat while the food is in front of them and starve when it goes away. They think the whole thing is out of their control. And I say that's okay for them as long as they're willing to pay the price. They go hungry for a few days, and it's pretty pathetic to watch them because they moan and groan and feel so sorry for themselves."

She inhaled a long, slow breath and let it out slowly before continuing.

"But storms during syzygies are different. Without caves, they're out on the beach without protection and it's not just a matter of being hungry for a few days. People have tried to help them. But the Krog Padders just won't—or can't—listen. As soon as everything's fine, they 'Happy be!' all day long and enjoy it."

Meato thought of Vortex back in Monterey. Vortex was like that. He was always so happy when they took him to the dog park or fed him or took him to the beach. He was thrilled when they threw him a ball and went hiking in the woods, where he picked up ticks. He was always so happy in the present moment and didn't think about the future at all.

Meato could hear the rain beginning to splatter on the ground outside the cave. How pleasant it was to just sit there and listen to it, his feet all toasty, the sweet smell of Krog Pad acorns wafting from the backpack, mixed with the urthy smell of rain.

A minute passed and then Meato suddenly raised his head, as if in recognition, and sat bolt upright.

He was just like Vortex, he realized. He always wanted to enjoy what was right in front of him. He never wanted to think about the next hour, much less the next day or week. He always put things off as long as he could. He twiddled his pencil and got lost in the moment while he was doing his homework instead of getting it done. In fact, for most of his short existence, he'd been entirely present! And wasn't that a gift? Isn't that why he was so special? *The gift of Presence?*

But then another thing occurred to him. And this one stung. His parents fed Vortex, bought him fun toys, and took him to the vet. His father had even built Vortex a fine doghouse by the sea. Vortex didn't need to worry about anything. And his parents took care of him, too, in the same way. They paid the mortgage, put food on the table, bought him video games and toys, and took him to the doctor when he got sick. His parents worried about his needs so he didn't have to.

Meato blinked. He'd been entirely blind. There was a *gift* to his *Presence*, all right, but there was also a cost! He was dependent on his parents completely, for everything. He had no power of his own. He was pathetic! And if he kept this up, he'd grow up ... well, he'd grow up to be just like Shum! *He'd grow up to be a Krog Padder!*

Meato looked at Ideth in panic.

"What happens to my duppies during storms at syzygies?" he demanded. "What happens to them, Ideth?!"

Ideth's eyes filled with tears.

"Have you ever noticed that the Krog Padders have so few children? They keep having them, so it's not the birth rate that's low. It's the *death* rate that's *high*, Meato. They lose their children in storms like this. The tides are just too strong in a storm surge. If they'd only build trails and maintain caves, here in the bluffs, they'd be safe—just like you and me. But they don't. They think if they simply ignore the future, it will never happen. That's why they cry '*No see! Not be!*' It's only when they actually *see* a storm on the horizon that they remember the danger. And the best they can do at that point is to squeeze their eyes shut and try to pretend *it's not going to happen*. That's what's going on down there on the beach, but it's too late now. The tides are in."

Meato whipped his head around to look at the mouth of the cave and then got up and raced to it. Looking out, under a dark sky boiling with clouds, with the rain falling in sheets, what he could see of the beach was all water churning, boiling, ugly water lapping, pushing, buffeting against the bluff as if to knock it free.

"IKTAE!" he screamed.

Chapter 21

SEARCH AND RECOVERY

I know that in many adventure stories, the hero would now dive into the roiling waves with a sword, slay a couple of sea monsters, and save his lady. But that's not going to happen here. Meato had no sword, urth has no sea monsters, and Iktae was just a child. Instead, he leapt into the treacherous ocean completely unprepared, and flailed about for nearly an hour, until he was mercifully flung back to Ideth by a mighty wave, and she put an end to his heroics. He resisted her tooth and nail, of course, determined to rescue Iktae at any cost, but it was no use. Having reached the far limit of human endurance, he had to face the terrible truth. He couldn't save Iktae. Not like this. She could be anywhere by now. So, with no other choice, he spent the night weeping and praying, just like his poor parents had wept and prayed for him. But unlike them, he wouldn't have to live with the *not knowing*. In the morning, he would find out what had happened to Iktae. That, at least, was a blessing.

The storm was a terrible one, and Ideth and Meato could see the damage as they looked down on the beach from their cave the next morning. Meato was all cried out, and felt terribly weak.

"Can you face it?" asked Ideth, taking his hand.

"I must," he replied. "But I'm sick with anger at myself. I should have seen this coming! I should have been able to save her."

Ideth had spent the night alternately holding and comforting Meato and neatly organizing her backpack. It now held emergency food, herbal medicines that she'd been cooking up the entire time she'd been on the Island, some bandages she'd picked up at the East End Paddling Station, and her sewing kit.

"Not made for sewing skin or blubber," she thought, "but it will do in a pinch."

The bluff was very slippery after the rains, and it took them almost an hour to get down to the beach safely. As they descended, they could see the washed up debris everywhere. Whole trees had been slammed onto the island by the storm surge, splintering like matches.

Slowly, over the course of the morning, the Krog Padders began appearing, in ones and twos, bedraggled, some bleeding, none of them "happy be." Meato didn't see any children, though the distraught parents were looking for them desperately, under the tree branches, in piles of sand, and up against the bluffs, where they might have been carried and crushed by the waves. Ideth tended to the more serious injuries, while Meato helped the Krog Padders in their searching. Mid-morning, Meato looked up and saw Shum rooting around the remains of the boat wreckage, looking for Iktae. Meato went over and put his arms around him.

"Iktae go," Shum said flatly. And then he wept on Meato's shoulder, drowning in shame.

Six children had been found by mid-afternoon: four dead, one near-death but hanging on with Ideth's help, and one miraculously alive.

But there was no sign of Iktae.

"Likely as not, she never knew what hit her," said Ideth to Meato, kindly. "The storm surge comes quickly—you saw that. She didn't suffer."

Meato stopped looking for Iktae and turned his attention to the living. Ideth had stepped off her judgmental perch and, just this once, felt sorry enough for the Krog Padders that she helped them gather food. Then she built a fire so she could cook for them.

"They won't cook for themselves," she told Meato grimly, "but they'll lap it up quickly enough if it's cooked for them."

She was right, as usual. The surviving Krog Padders gathered around Ideth's campfire, sniffing the air. But it wasn't a "Happy be!" kind of sniffing. It was a downcast, shame-filled sniffing that made Meato want to slap them.

"YOU DID THIS TO YOUR OWN CHILDREN!" he wanted to scream, but it seemed too cruel.

They were lying in their own bed, as Ideth would say. They were paying the price for their own folly.

"The problem is that they won't learn from it," said Ideth at sunset.

Meato had already heard a couple of his duppies shout "Happy be!" and had to agree.

"It's disgusting," he grumbled, poking at the fire with a branch from one of the washed-up trees. "I see how completely disgusting it is, but I still like them. Somehow, I still like them."

Ideth smiled knowingly.

"Our time on Krog Pad Island is done," she said. "And so is your time on Urth. Look at the color of your fingers. They're almost back to their creamy brown, just like the rest of you. That's the sign that you're ready to go home. Earth is drawing you back."

Meato looked at his fingers. They were no longer lavender. Instead, they were a weird color somewhere between lavender and light brown that reminded him of the color of Vortex' poop more than anything else.

"We'll get ourselves packed up in the morning, paddle back to the East Ender," Ideth continued, "and then head for Returning Island the next day. Your parents in Monterey have been missing you."

"I miss them too," said Meato, suddenly realizing that he missed them a great deal. In fact, he was suddenly homesick and couldn't wait to see them.

"Glad to hear it," replied Ideth. "It's been nearly six months and you're a different Meato than the Mateo that I found. You're a fantastic climber now for one thing, and a good cook. You were a wonderful big brother to Iktae, too, before she died too soon. You cared for her. You know you did."

Meato nodded. He felt the fresh pain of losing Iktae, but he couldn't help but imagine how astonished everyone would be when he got home. He was sure he would make the

climbing team at the Spidering Up Rock Gym this year and maybe even go to nationals. A fantasy of himself scrambling effortlessly up a rock gym wall, with adoring fans screaming beneath him, made him smile, despite how difficult the day had been. And he imagined whipping up dinner his first night home, his parents smelling the delicious food, their eyes wide open in amazement.

"Well done, findling," said Ideth. "Keep holding onto your imagination. It's your gift, Meato. It's your *real* sword. But now it's tempered with self-reliance, caring about others, and an understanding of how important it is to plan for the future. It's a mighty sword, Meato. Wield it well."

By mid-morning the next day, Ideth and Meato were standing on the beach, saying good-bye to his duppies. "Happy sea!" shouted several of them cheerily, giving the Krog Padder version of 'Bon Voyage!' Meato could see they were already in an improved mood from the night before.

Meato kept looking around for Shum but he didn't appear.

"Probably too ashamed," he thought. But after he'd said his farewells to everyone and was about to put on his snorkel, he saw Shum in the distance, bounding up the beach, at a gallop.

"Happy be! Happy be!" Shum cried with unabashed, unbridled joy. "Wait for we! Wait for we!"

Meato turned to Ideth with a roll of his eyes that said, "Good grief, is he over the storm and the loss of his daughter already?"

But Ideth didn't return it. Instead, she was smiling with a light in her eyes. And everyone began cheering then, jumping up and down in such a flurry of excitement and glee that Meato wondered what could have possibly come over them.

Then his eyes opened wide and he understood.

Shum was carrying Iktae. And she was all in one piece, looking a little bedraggled and worse for wear, but carrying the cover of a book in her hand, holding it up for Meato and Ideth to see.

"The Good Urth!" she said, triumphantly, as Shum eased her down onto the sand. "I find it on the beach after storm!"

Meato dissolved into relief and ran to her. "We! We! We!" he cried, embracing her tightly and then whirling her about him.

She clung to his neck and laughed, but when he released her, she whispered: "I safe, Meato. I climb up bluff." She pointed to a spot near where the Krog Padders had been standing before the storm. "No more *'No see, not be.'* I be free!"

Meato was ecstatic! He'd rescued Iktae after all! She'd climbed the bluff, following his example, because *he* climbed with such confidence and skill. In her time of greatest need, she'd put her faith in *him* because he'd been so good to her. She trusted him! And although he was leaving Urth now and would never see her again, he felt better than he ever thought he would or could. He'd saved a life—the life of an extraordinary girl who would do great things with it, he was sure—and he couldn't help but admire the hero that he was.

Chapter 22

ELVIA

Ideth and Meato reached the East End Paddling Station well before dark. They were checked in by an elderly gentleman named Mot who couldn't hear very well and seemed a bit confused.

"Two berths, one uppy and one findling," he said, peering at his guest roster uncertainly. "I'll put you in the Shark Room. Dinner's included for findlings. But you, madam," he said, removing his glasses and looking respectfully at Ideth, "your stay is entirely free, of course. We won't charge the Uppy Council a single Cairntip tidbit. We're honored to have you as a guest."

Ideth and Meato made their way down to the Shark Room, but when they arrived they found that it was already occupied. From inside, they could hear a child sobbing and the voice of a woman who was trying to reason with her.

"But it's no good!" cried the child. "I hate this room. It's ugly!"

"It's the room they assigned us, Elvia, and it's only for one night," the woman replied. "Come here now and let me wipe those tears off your face." Then she added, "Can you find a color for the feeling?"

Ideth pulled Meato away from the door.

"Clearly the wrong room," she whispered. "Let's go fix the mistake."

They climbed back up the ladder to the reception area and explained the error to Mot.

"Hmmm," he said, scratching his mop of stunning white hair. "Guess I already gave the Shark Room to that other uppy and her findling. Gets confusing when we have more than one set at the same time. But we still have the Mermaid Room."

He winked at Meato.

"Not a good room for most boys," he chuckled, as he handed them the key.

Meato looked at Ideth and Ideth looked at Meato. Clearly, they were thinking the same thing.

Ideth cleared her throat.

"You know," she said, "I think the other uppy/findling pair might be willing to switch. Have they been here long?"

"Not long enough to settle in, if that's what you mean," replied Mot. "I'll go talk to them and see what they say."

Mot disappeared down the hole and Meato looked through to the dining room. The same sign still announced the dinner arrangements: "Dinner served promptly at seven. Loincloths respectfully suggested."

"Did you notice the owl?" Ideth asked with a smirk. "They've replaced it with a plastic gull-eating dolphin. Looks ridiculous."

Mot returned with a smile on his face.

"You just made a little girl very happy!" he told them. "They're packing up now and I've given them the key to the Mermaid Room. As soon as they're gone, you can move yourself in. Here's the key to the Shark Room."

Ideth and Meato waited a respectful 10 minutes before returning to the belly of the hotel. The door to the Shark Room was cracked open, and inside there was a very neatly printed note, written in a girl's hand.

"Thank you!" it said, in frilly letters. The point in the exclamation point was in the shape of a heart.

"Sweet note," said Ideth. And then she looked around. "Goodness! I can see why she didn't want to stay here. *Yuk!*"

Meato's reaction was completely different. He gaped with pleasure and wonder. There were murals of dozens of different sharks on the walls, only some of which he'd ever seen in picture books. But the crowning glory of the room, and the one that Ideth's eyes were riveted on, was an enormous Great Purple, crushing a bloody urthling between its mighty jaws, guts and blood splashed everywhere.

"Wow!" cried Meato with obvious delight. "This is perfect! And the berths are made to look like they're in the Great Purple's stomach."

Ideth got busy unpacking, while Meato snooped around.

"I'd like the bottom berth, Ideth, if that's okay. It's got a pull out drawer beneath it that's full of shark-themed jigsaw puzzles. There's a board that you can pull down to work on them in bed, and you can push it back up when you're ready to sleep. The puzzle stays in one piece until you're ready to work on it again. It's so cool!"

"Well, we got here early, so you'll have time for a puzzle," said Ideth. "I just hope there aren't any pieces missing. I hate that."

While Meato chose a puzzle, Ideth wandered out into the hallway and down to the Mermaid Room. She knocked.

A bright-eyed earth girl opened the door. She beamed at Ideth and said, "Welcome to the Mermaid Room! Are you an uppy?"

"Yes," Ideth replied. "And who are you?"

"I'm Elvia," she said. "And I just lost a tooth!" She opened her mouth wide to show Ideth the bloody hole.

Ideth smiled. "I remember how it feels to lose a tooth. You can run your tongue right into the soft spot. It hurts but it also feels kind of good."

"That's right," the girl said, pushing her tongue into the bloody space. "Lacie says urth children get real gold when they lose a tooth. All I have to do is put the tooth in this little bag around my neck."

She held out the small, elegant bag for Ideth's inspection.

"Ah, ha!" Ideth exclaimed. "Well, Lacie is right. And there she is now! How are you, dear?"

"Ideth!" cried a tall, stunningly-beautiful urth woman. She was elegantly dressed and had amazing eyes the color of blue sea glass and a mane of yellow hair that fell gracefully to her slender waist. "Are you on your way in or on your way out?"

"Out," replied Ideth, "and it was an unqualified success. Wonderful boy. Gift of *Presence*."

"We're coming in," said Lacie. "On our way to Amdar."

Ideth nodded. "The gift of *Feeling Deeply*," she thought. "That will be a challenge."

Elvia twirled around the room like a ballerina.

"This room is fantastic!" she said sweeping her hands in a wide arc. Mermaids, swathed in pink and gold, bathed the walls of the room. There was a dainty vanity table with a huge mirror, a pretend mermaid cave, and a wand.

"That's a wonderful feeling, Elvia!" said Lacie, encouragingly. "Can you color it up?"

Elvia ran across the room and picked up something that looked like a picture book. Then she flipped through it, cocking her head to one side, considering.

"Pink," she said. "Pink Bubbles." Then she looked up at Lacie questioningly, as if seeking her approval.

"I just hope she doesn't have a tantrum at dinner," Lacie said to Ideth under her breath. "She was in a very dark mood earlier."

Ideth gave Lacie's arm a pinch. "You *chose* that stripe," she reminded her teasingly. "You're well-trained. You can handle it."

Ideth said good-bye and returned to the Shark Room. Meato was putting together a particularly gory puzzle, depicting a sailor spearing a Tiger Shark through the eye.

"Good," she thought, "It has 500 pieces. That should keep him busy until dinnertime and give me some time for a nap. We'll be up early tomorrow."

Ideth climbed the ladder to the top berth, enjoying the luxury of knowing she wouldn't be banging her head on the berth above her. She looked out of the porthole. It wasn't dark yet, and the sea was green and gold in the filtered sunlight. Several colorful reef fishes darted past, showing off their yellows and bright blues.

She sighed and let her body completely relax, feeling the gentle rocking rhythm of the station. It was so satisfying to have found and trained another child. And now she could go back to Cairntip for a while, spend a few days cleaning and organizing her cave, and then sink into the bliss of repositioning, an uppy's version of vacation. What fun! She was planning out the details already.

The dining room was packed. Meato and Ideth got there a bit early, and their side of the table was already full by the time Elvia and Lacie got there. Elvia looked angry and glowered at her plate. Lacie sat beside her, talking to her in a low tone.

"That's the other findling, isn't it?" Meato asked Ideth as the food was being served.

"Yes," she replied. "She has the gift of *Feeling Deeply*."

Meato smiled across at Elvia, encouragingly. He knew what it was like to be new on Urth and unsure of what was going to happen next. But Elvia seemed to be afraid of him, or possibly in awe, and barely looked up.

When Meato and Ideth got back to the Shark Room, it was dark. Meato had only about 30 puzzle pieces to go and eagerly asked Ideth to help him finish.

"You go ahead and complete it," she said. "I think I'm going to hit the ducky sack early."

"Pleeeze?" pleaded Meato, a glint in his eye. "I could really use your help."

Ideth relented and helped him finish the puzzle. But when they got to the last piece, it was missing.

"Is it on the floor?" asked Meato, leaning over and inspecting beneath the berth. Ideth looked under the puzzle box and slid her hand between the bedding and the berth board. Nothing.

"Oh, I hate this," she muttered. "I always seem to get the puzzles with pieces missing. And darned if it isn't just one piece this time. Frustrating!"

Meato grinned, reached under his pillow, and pulled out the final piece.

"Gotcha!" he said, as he slipped it in place.
It was the shark's pierced, bloody eye.

Chapter 23

THE RETURNING

"A returning is much easier than a finding," Ideth explained, before they geared up and set out the next morning. It was early and the ocean was calm and inviting. "For one thing, there's no Finding Fruit, thank goodness. For another, it takes much less time. You'll be back in Monterey, hugging your parents, before you know it."

Meato was excited, but also sad at having to leave Ideth behind.

"You could come with me and meet my parents!" he said eagerly. "They'd love you!"

"I'm sure I'd love them too, my findling, but things just don't work that way. It's bittersweet, but our time together is over. You've been fully found now, and you need to return to your family. The training of an unseen child has a beginning and an end. Today is the end. But you'll be in my heart when I wake every morning and again in my heart when I go to sleep every night. We're connected that way now, and always will be."

Meato sighed. "So what happens now?" he asked. "Where do we go?"

"Returning Island," she said. "Half a day's paddle with no stops needed. We've had an excellent breakfast and we'll be fine. The buoy is all stocked, sealed, and ready to go. We can always snack along the way if we get desperate."

Meato remembered their lunch in the ocean on the way to the East End Paddling Station from Finding Island. He hoped to avoid a repeat performance of that watery, messy experience. It was hard to believe that his journey "in" had been only six months before. It seemed like a lifetime. Now he was on his way "out."

"Will my parents even recognize me?" he wondered. "What will I tell them about where I've been? How can I possibly explain it? They'll think I've gone nuts and put me in a mental hospital."

"Those things will take care of themselves," Ideth assured him. "Trust me."

Paddling with Ideth again was lovely. The *thrust, thrust, float* was peaceful and soothing. The tingling along his skin while she was navigating felt familiar rather than strange. The sea creatures were beautiful. He even saw two huge yellow lobsters that appeared to be fiercely protecting their turf. The weather was calm. There was no wind.

Every now and then, Ideth surfaced to breathe and they looked around. Just before noon, they surfaced for the last time.

"There!" said Ideth, pointing to a low island, covered with trees. "That's Returning Island. Not much to look at, but you won't be there long."

They said good-bye on the beach. Meato retrieved his original clothes from the buoy and changed into them, while Ideth looked the other way.

"I'm done," said Meato. He put his loincloth, wetsuit, mask, and snorkel in a heap on the sand. It was the last time he'd see them.

Ideth turned around and looked him up and down with approval.

"Those clothes are almost worn out," she said, "and too small for you now. You've grown at least two inches since you arrived and you're stronger than an ox."

Meato smiled at the compliment.

"I love you, Ideth. Not the way I love Iktae but in another, very special way. If I could have two mothers, I'd choose you as my second."

"I'll always be your Urth mother," said Ideth. "And I'll take care of Iktae. I'll take her to Cairntip so she can get educated. It's against the rules, but I'll convince the Uppy Council somehow. Then she can return to Krog Pad Island and teach her people, so they won't keep losing their children to the storms."

"Thank you," Meato said, his eyes brimming with tears. They hugged.

"Well done, my findling. Now go into the forest and the returning will happen all by itself."

Meato walked toward the trees, and when he reached them, he looked back. His last image of Ideth was of her waving to him from the beach, the buoy and his abandoned paddling gear beside her. She looked happy for him.

He didn't know what to do. Ideth had given him no instructions. He had no food, no water, and no ducky sack.

The island was unusually quiet, just like Finding Island, but the trees were different. They were much taller and bore no fruit. After a few minutes of wandering around, he stopped beside one of the tallest trees and looked up into its silver-gray branches. It was easily as tall as the tallest trees on Earth, the redwoods he'd seen in Muir Woods, on a family vacation.

"I'm going to climb that," he thought. "Because if I do, I'll be able to see the whole island!"

It was difficult, to be sure. The wood was slippery, apparently from a recent rain, and he had trouble getting a grip on the smooth bark. Before he'd come to Urth, he never would have tried it. But he had decent muscles and plenty of climbing experience now, and he wasn't afraid. Branch after branch, he crawled his way up, ever-closer to the bright and view-promising blue sky peeking through the canopy high above.

"I can climb this tree," he told himself, with a confidence born from the many mornings he'd spent climbing the bluffs on Krog Pad Island. "I can climb this tree and see what this island is like."

And sure enough, when Meato finally eased himself onto the highest branch and stood up, he could see everything.

Returning Island, it turned out, was almost perfectly round, blanketed with a magnificent, fruit-free, silvery Returning Forest. And the stately trees were holding hands, or so it seemed to him, swaying together in the gusty ocean breeze, as if waving good-bye.

Meato looked over his shoulder to see the 360 degree panorama, and something caught his eye. It was another

low-lying, forested island nearby, glinting purple in the sun, like an amethyst.

"It's Finding Island!" he cried. "Oh, how I wish I had a cell phone, or even a chatterbox, so I could take a photo for my mom."

It was Meato's final thought on Urth, and I think we can agree it was a sweet one. But it came and went quickly, for he was suddenly drawn back home, never to return.

Tingle! Zap! Siphon! Noodle! Freeze! Gasp! Swell! In the blink of an eye the Returning Forest had vanished, and Meato was crossing the airless void of outer space again, on a journey that would liberate his anguished family from their terrible loss and poor Jimmy Albini from a life in prison.

A galaxy of suns, billions of them with planets like Earth and Urth, streaked past in only 28.7 seconds. "If only I could visit them all one day!" he thought briefly, as they whizzed by.

And then, with a crushing deceleration and an unceremonious little plop, Meato (now Mateo again) found himself breathless and wide-eyed, lying on his bed in Monterey, staring up at the crack in the ceiling that had started his adventure so many months before.

Chapter 24

HOMECOMING

O fficer Morgan was sitting at the desk in his small office at the police station. His office had a tiny window that was broken in three places, the result of an accident, years before, when some kids had slammed into the building with a car. The glass had never been fixed, and it reminded Officer Morgan, every time he happened to see it, how little money his department had to spend. If he'd only chosen a different line of work, he might own a fine house by the sea. Instead, he lived with his nagging wife in a run-down cottage two blocks away.

It was a busy day, as all his days were, and he was buried under a pile of paperwork. People think that police officers spend their days running around doing exciting things like driving in high speed car chases and arresting people on the FBI's 10 Most Wanted List. Officer Morgan had thought so too, when he was a boy, and that's why he'd decided to become a policeman. But the sad reality was that he spent most of his time filling out reports.

He had four large binders open on his desk that day, stacks of disorganized papers under them, a desk calendar below that, and at the very bottom, a squashed cinnamon roll that he'd bought for breakfast more than three months earlier. He'd put it down on his desk when he'd been called into his boss' office for a meeting (having to do with a late report) and had forgotten about it. Now, it was in the early stages of fossilization.

Officer Morgan was typing up a report on his computer, and drinking his third cup of coffee for the day, when his cell phone rang. A breathless, excited voice spoke to him from the other end of the line.

"Officer Morgan, Mateo is HOME!" cried Mateo's mother in a frantic voice. "He simply walked into the kitchen while I was making lunch. Roberto and I just can't BELIEVE IT! You need to come RIGHT NOW!"

Officer Morgan knew Mrs. Marino's voice instantly and just about fell off his chair.

"WHAT?!" he exploded, leaping up and upsetting his coffee. "What the heck are you SAYING?"

"I'm telling you, MATEO IS HOME! He's safe. I don't know how, but he's HOME."

"We'll be right there!" Officer Morgan cried, dropping his cell phone and staring at it in disbelief.

I just finished telling you that Officer Morgan found his job dull, but this day was going to be an exception. He sprinted out of his office into the break room, where several other police officers were making coffee and getting ready for what they thought was going to be another dull, boring day too.

"MATEO MARINO HAS BEEN FOUND!" he shouted. "HE'S *ALIVE*! I just got a call from his mother. He's at their house!"

There was a stunned silence.

"Are you sure?" responded one of the officers, her eyes widening as she gasped audibly.

"I haven't seen him, but unless his mother has gone crazy, YES!"

The station became a flurry of activity after that. Everyone had to be told, a team of officers needed to be dispatched to the Marino home, and someone had the good sense to contact Social Services and get a child trauma psychologist involved. It wouldn't be long before the media would get a whiff of the story and then all heck would break loose.

They decided not to turn on their sirens. They didn't want to attract any more attention to the situation than necessary. Three police cars and an ambulance arriving at the Marino home simultaneously was certain to arouse the curiosity of their neighbors and, sure enough, Amber Duncan, who lived two doors down, saw them arrive and walked outside to see what all the fuss was about.

Soon, many of the Marino's neighbors had wandered out into the street and were talking to one another excitedly. Within 20 minutes of the officers' arrival, one of them had called Channel 12.

Mateo was in remarkably good shape for a boy who had supposedly been abducted and nearly murdered. His clothes were too small for him and rather frayed, but they also appeared to have been carefully mended in several places. His mental state seemed excellent, too. When the officers walked in the door, Mateo was being hug-squashed by his ecstatic father, and Vortex was racing around the house, leaping and barking with glee.

No one asked him what had happened. The child psychologist was firm about that.

"He'll give us the story in his own time," she told his family. "Right now, he needs to be looked over by the paramedics to make sure he's okay, and then they'll transport him to the hospital for a more thorough examination. As long as he's in no imminent danger, we'll release him to you in a few hours. You can stay with him the entire time. I know you won't want him out of your sight."

They all nodded, tears streaming down their faces. They'd been crying with joy ever since Mateo had come home.

The psychologist also prepared them for what was about to happen to their lives.

"You've been in the eyes of the media before, so you know what it's like. They'll be hounding you from the moment this gets out. I suggest you let the police do the talking on your behalf, and Mateo mustn't be allowed to talk to them at all. This is an ongoing criminal investigation and it's important that he talks only to you and the police."

She squatted down to look Alex directly in the eyes.

"You may be excited and want to text your friends and put this all up on Facebook, but you can't do that until we get this sorted out. Okay? I need your word on that, little buddy."

Alex nodded solemnly, looking up at his parents.

"It'll be okay," said his father, ruffling his hair. "We'll help you through this."

It was several hours before they were home from the hospital. Mateo slept between his ecstatic parents that night, something he hadn't done since he was a very young child. But it felt so wonderful to have them on both sides, snuggling him and breaking out in sobs of gratitude every minute or so, that he wouldn't have wanted to be anywhere else.

"I'm home, Ideth," he thought, hoping she could read his mind from the other side of the galaxy. "I'm home and I'm loved. They see me now."

"I know, little findling," he was sure he heard her answer. "Well done. You'll have a wonderful life. You'll see that I'm right."

Chapter 25

J. O. ALBINI
WRITES A BOOK

"**W**hat did it feel like when you knew you were going to be released?" asked Maria Thomson, the tanned, toothy, and beautifully attired host of Good Day Monterey. Her long legs were crossed and disappeared seamlessly into shoes made of fine Italian leather that were the same color as her skin.

Jimmy Oscar Albini, a microphone clipped to his lapel, smiled sheepishly.

"It felt good," he said.

Jimmy was obviously a man of few words, which made him a terrible guest on Maria's show. "This will be difficult," she thought.

There was a silence, which Maria quickly swooped in to fill.

"I'm sure you must have felt better than just good," she suggested, smiling at him encouragingly. "You were over the moon with joy, no doubt!"

The camera swung from her to Jimmy.

"Yes," said Jimmy.

Another silence.

"What was the first thing you did when you got back home?" Maria asked, leaning forward with fake interest. "I'll bet you hugged your family pretty hard."

Jimmy winced. Actually, the first thing he'd done was to go to the bathroom. But he couldn't say that on air. And he didn't have a family, so that hardly applied.

More silence.

"Well," said Maria, casting a sympathetic glance to the camera. "Maybe you'd like to keep those precious moments to yourself, Jimmy. I think I would in your position."

Jimmy flooded with relief and Maria changed her approach.

"So what's next?" she asked brightly.

"A book," Jimmy said.

He'd had publishers hounding him ever since he'd been released and had multiple offers of deals linked to dollar figures so high that he had trouble comprehending them.

"A BOOK!" cried Maria brightly. "Wow, Jimmy, that's fantastic! I'm sure our listeners would love to hear your story. An upstanding citizen accused of a horrible crime that he didn't commit, languishing in jail for months awaiting trial."

Her forehead wrinkled in concern. "Then convicted, and suddenly released!" Her eyebrows sprang upward. "If that's not bestseller material," she said, smiling directly into the camera, "I don't know what is!"

Jimmy squirmed. He'd been the center of attention for weeks now and most of it felt wonderful. Everyone was being nice to him. His boss had offered him his old job back, told

reporters that Jimmy was the best worker he'd ever had, and thrown him a huge party.

Sarah and her sisters had cleaned his apartment until it shone, and then hung curtains. He got mail from all over the world and most of it sat, unopened, beside his mail box, because the outpouring of sympathy and congratulations was so overwhelming.

But the media was simply a pain. He could see right through their tactics and found them shameful. He'd only agreed to this interview to get them off his back.

Maria began again. "Do you have a title yet?" she asked. "Our listeners will want to know so they can buy it when it comes out."

"*The Art of Roofing*," said Jimmy.

Maria frowned and appeared to be terribly disappointed. Why would a man like Jimmy Albini write a book about roofing when he could write one about his terrible ordeal and make a fortune?

Jimmy saw the look on her face, but he didn't care. His book wouldn't be written for people like Maria, so what did it matter? He already had the chapters laid out in his mind.

After the show was over, Jimmy was escorted to the front door of the studio by a knock-dead gorgeous young woman who whispered, "You did great in there. Maria is such an exploitative prig."

Jimmy laughed and they talked for several more minutes in front of the studio. Lila was an artist and was only working at the studio to save up enough money to take a year off.

"I want to paint," she said. "It's all I ever do in my free time, so I figure I should take a shot at making it my living. But I need to build up a bigger portfolio."

Jimmy told her about his job as a roofer and explained that carpentry was a kind of art as well.

"You look at the job and you think, 'How could I make this roof last longer? How can I make sure it never leaks again?' There are so many slip-shod companies out there. They use cheap materials and cut corners all over the place. We don't do that at Bob's Roofing. We like to do things well."

"Yes, I do too," Lila thought to herself. "I like this guy."

And then a very odd thing happened. Jimmy asked Lila out on a date, and she accepted. A few years later, when they were married and had a daughter on the way, Jimmy told her that he wasn't even scared when he did it.

"I felt so much better about myself that it never crossed my mind that you'd say no," he told her. "It's funny what a little self-respect does for a person."

The Art of Roofing sold very well, partly because Jimmy's exoneration had made him a celebrity, and partly because it wasn't just about roofing.

"When you find a leak, try to figure out what caused it," he wrote on page 22, "not just how to fix it. Because if you don't address the cause, it will just leak again."

Jimmy might have been talking about his own life, or the lives of all the other young men he'd known in prison. If a judge had just taken the time to find out *why* they committed crimes, not just how to punish them, he might have prevented

them from becoming lifelong criminals. He'd been lucky that a judge gave him a second chance at age 19, allowing him to fix the leak in his own life for good.

But Shrimp, and many others like him, would spend their lives locked away, their potential wasted. Maybe one of them could have mastered a craft like he had, or even written a bestseller.

Jimmy also had hidden advice for parents, even though it still sounded like he was talking about roofs.

"Every roof is different," Jimmy told them on page 98, "and special in its own way. The owner knows his roof better than you do because he lives under it. And you won't know how to help him make his roof as strong as it can be unless you listen."

Chapter 26

THE FORGETTING

We're nearly at the end of this story, as you've probably figured out by now because this is the last chapter. But there's one important, very important, thing I have yet to tell you.

If you're ever in Monterey and run into Mateo, you won't be able to ask him about his adventures. Nor will you be able to ask his parents, or Alex, or Jimmy Albini, or Officer Morgan about the six months that Mateo was missing. You see, something very odd happens soon after a fully found child returns from an adventure on Urth. He forgets all about it. And his parents forget about their trauma and pain, and everyone else forgets about their role in what happened.

Everyone forgets, but everyone's been changed forever, too.

Mateo's parents will no longer scold him for being lazy and self-absorbed. They won't remember why their attitude toward him has changed. Instead they'll simply have discovered, deep down inside, that their children are the most important part of their lives and that ignoring who they are is almost as bad as losing them forever.

They'll enroll Mateo in a special school that encourages and nurtures imagination, and he will thrive. Then, when he's a teenager, he'll begin to write stories, working hard at crafting good tales, even though it will be hard sometimes. And he'll take many risks, sending his stories to publishers, facing possible rejection. Most importantly, he'll think ahead and make plans, finding his way into a future of his own choosing.

He'll never lose his gift of *Presence*. He'll use it to make a difference in the world. And in the end, he'll become a widely beloved author of children's books, a writer whose imagination is heralded as extraordinary.

He'll have two dogs, Ideth and Iktae, strange names to be sure, and ones he won't be able to explain to anyone, or even to himself. But he'll never forget to feed them, and they'll live long and happy lives.

Jimmy Albini won't be able to recall exactly why he had been at the TV studio when he met Lila, but he will build up a nice nest-egg from the sales of his book and will start a roofing company of his own called Second-Chance Roof Repairs. True to his gift of *Liking to do Things Well*, he'll sit on the board of a non-profit organization that helps troubled teenagers get a leg up, offering them jobs at his roofing company without any incentive from the government.

Alex's experience with losing Mateo will make him a more cautious child, a little more withdrawn than before, which will save his life when he's 16 years old, because he'll round the corner in his parent's car a little more slowly than he would have otherwise, and miss the truck with the drunk driver, who will wander too far into the wrong lane.

Officer Morgan, who witnessed the miraculous recovery of a child who'd been missing for half a year, will realize there's more to life than staying in a secure job that makes you feel unhappy and overwhelmed. He'll retire from the police force early and move back to his home town in upstate New York, where he and his wife will reconnect and begin to enjoy each other's company for the first time in years.

But Ideth and everyone on Urth will remember what happened. And if you ever find yourself on Urth, you can ask Ideth all the questions you might have about the details of this story that you can't ask Mateo. ("Is there an Octopus Room at the East End Paddling Station?" for example.)

Who knows? Maybe you'll be going to Urth yourself soon, to have your own adventure. Or perhaps you have been there already and forgotten all about it.

THE END

Like this book and want more from this author?
Visit www.SpinningWheelPress.com and join the Insider's Club for **FREE** book giveaways, coupons, audio flipbooks, announcements of upcoming book releases, and much, much more!

Synopsis of
Elvia and the Gift of Feeling Deeply:

Earl and Sally Hill are reluctant to take their feisty nine-year-old daughter Elvia on vacation to Tanzania, Africa. But she's so moody that they can't find anyone to babysit her, so they take her along anyway, hoping for the best.

Unfortunately, their worst fears come true. Elvia disappears from Tembo National Park, apparently the victim of a lion snatching! A massive search ensues, involving a corrupt park director, a delusional lion expert, a witchdoctor, and a compassionate couple who run a non-profit organization called Parents of Swallowed Children.

But Elvia isn't in the belly of a lion. She's on a planet called Urth, on the other side of the galaxy, with a beautiful "uppy" named Lacie who takes her on a delightful voyage aboard a cruising submarine to a mysterious island called Amdar. Along the way, Elvia meets a 10-year-old boy with the unlikely name of Rats, who is also from Earth and shares an exciting secret. And she learns, too, that she has an amazing and powerful gift: the gift of *Feeling Deeply*.

Taming and channeling her gift is Elvia's great challenge, and in a tiny room at the top of the Amdar Lighthouse, she begins her training. But will she finish it in time to save Rats from a terrible catastrophe? And, in the end, will she be allowed to return to Earth to end her parents' nightmare? Or will she be trapped forever on Amdar, unable to find her way home?

Future Books in the
Tales by Moons-Light™ Series:

Elvia and the Gift of Feeling Deeply
Bubba and the Gift of Big Thoughts
How Piper Found Peace
Timmy and the Rock from Star

About the Author

Ruthy Ballard is a scientist, artist, and children's book author who lives and works in Sacramento, California. By day, she is "Dr. Ruth Ballard," a professor and forensic biologist who serves as a consultant in criminal cases involving DNA evidence. By night, she romps in an imaginative world of color and words that has been her playground since childhood.

Ruthy is the author of *Mateo and the Gift of Presence* and is currently working on four other books in her "Tales by Moons-Light™" series: *Elvia and the Gift of Feeling Deeply*, *Bubba and the Gift of Big Thoughts*, *How Piper Found Peace*, and *Timmy and the Rock from Star*.

Ruthy's books are for middle grade readers (9-12), but her creative ventures don't stop there. She is also an artist whose unique creations aim to delight and inspire the adult crowd.

Ruthy is married to a musician, Ernie Hills, and is the mother of two sons, three cats, and a Samoyed dog named Mush, all of whom appear in her stories, in various guises, from time to time.

For more information about Ruthy and her creative endeavors, log onto www.SpinningWheelPress.com. Enjoy!